U0034540

會展
實用英語

（聽說口譯篇）

吳雲 主編

崧燁文化

目錄

Chapter 1
Enquiring about Holding a Conference 會議諮詢

Chapter 2
Booking an Event 招展商會展預訂

Chapter 3
Event Planning and Budgeting 會展策劃與預算

Chapter 4
Providing Exhibit Information 提供展覽資訊

Chapter 5
Visiting Foreign Exhibitors 拜會贊助商

Chapter 6
Negotiating on Exhibiting Space 展位談判

Chapter 7
Hiring A Stand 申請展位

Chapter 8
Personal Sales Calls 銷售拜訪（電話）

Chapter 9
Hiring People and Loaning Properties 租借物品 / 租用人員

Chapter 10
Safety and Security Service 安保服務

Chapter 11
Helping with Post-Conference Logistics 會後物流服務

Chapter 12
Opening and Reception 開幕與酒會

Chapter13
Attending the Event 參加展會

Chapter 14
Reserving Post Conference Tours 會後旅遊預訂

Chapter 15
Event Review Meetings 會後總結

Chapter 1
Enquiring about Holding a Conference 會議諮詢

▌Section 1 Listening Activities

Go over the following words and expressions before listening to the tape.

fund raising gala			募捐晚會
rehearsal		n.	排演
Murphy's law			墨菲法則
set aside			留出
so what			那又怎麼樣
sponsor		n.	贊助者
financial outlay			經濟支出
preliminary		A.	初期的，開始的
clearly defined responsibility			職責明確
indispensable		A.	不可缺少的

A. Spot Dictation

Designing and producing an event—whether it be a meeting, corporate event, (1)_____ gala, (2)_____, convention, (3)_____ or other special event—have been compared to a directing a movie but is actually more like a (4)_____. It is a high-wire act without the safety nets. Once your event starts there are no (5)_____. It's done in one take and there are no dress rehearsals. You are simply not able to (6)_____ —as you can from a movie script—of how your guests and suppliers will (7)_____. But (8)_____. Any event, whether it's for 50 or more than 2,000, (9)_____. Never forget Murphy's Law: (10)_____.

B. Multiple Choices

Directions: *In this section you will hear several Dialogues. After each Dialogue, there are some questions. Listen to the Dialogues carefully and choose the most* *appropriate answer to each question from the four choices marked A, B, C and D.*

● **Dialogue 1**

1. What's the purpose of the product launch?

    A. To invite some customers to hold a party.

    B. To Increase the sale of the new product.

    C. To investigate the sale of the new product.

    D. To decide how much money is needed to promote the new product.

2. What should be decided before an event is put into practice according to the Dialogue?

    A. The number of the customers being invited.

    B. The amount of money being set aside.

    C. Dates and venue of the event.

    D. The objective and budget.

● **Dialogue 2**

3. What is it that makes the woman go in a hurry?

    A. The exhibition.

    B. The equipment and facilities of the exhibition.

    C. The weather report.

    D. The storm.

4. What can be inferred from the Dialogue?

    A. Many external factors such as the local laws and even weather will have an effect on the success of an event.

    B. The equipment and facilities of an exhibition should be taken Good care of.

    C. An exhibition employee should listen to the weather forecast from time to time.

    D. Exhibition employees should cooperate with each other.

● **Dialogue 3**

5. What are the major responsibilities of an event-planning manager?

    A. To give advice and consultation about an event.

B. To estimate the preliminary cost of an event.

C. To manage everything well in order to ensure the success of an event.

D. To have a talk with the sponsor of the event.

6. What should be decided in the first place before an event is held?

　A. The sponsor.

　B. The goal and the budget

　C. The internal and external factors.

　D. The event committee.

7. Which of the following may NOT necessarily be considered when an event is being planned?

　A. The targeted audience.

　B. The location.

　C. The transportation.

　D. The local municipal government.

8. What requirements should an effective event team meet to ensure a successful event?

　A. It should be staffed with some professionals.

　B. It should match the skills and areas of interest to the areas of responsibilities.

　C. Each member should keep in mind clearly his (her) responsibility and cooperate with others.

　D. Every member of the team supports the manager.

● Dialogue 4

9. What questions are interviewees asked in the survey?

　A. What are the best channels for demonstrating products and services?

　B. Are exhibitions the most efficient way to do business?

　C. What are the best channels for building relationships with customers and prospects?

　D. Both A and C.

10. What conclusion can be drawn from the survey?

　A. Exhibitions have been considered as the most efficient way to do one-stop business.

　B. For many companies, exhibitions have become inseparable from their business.

C. Companies have been Increasingly aware of the importance of meetings and exhibitions.

D. All of the above.

11. According to the Dialogue, why can a trade faire be effective for businesses?

A. There are top-level buyers.

B. There are major players in the industry.

C. There is a most direct contact between the exhibitors and attendees.

D. Attendees can ask questions directly.

12. All meetings and exhibitions are not successful because_____.

A. The MICE industry is a promising industry.

B. Even the smallest fault in various factors will influence the effect.

C. More and more companies are involved in event-planning.

D. It's hard to control the number of event planners and attendees.

C. Passage Dictation

Directions: *In this section, you will hear a passage. Listen carefully and write down what you have heard on the tape.*

_____

_____

_____

_____

_____

_____

_____

_____

_____

_____

Tape script & Answers

A. Spot Dictation

Designing and producing an event—whether it be a meeting, corporate event, (1)<u>fund-raising</u> gala, (2)<u>conference</u>, convention, (3)<u>Incentive</u> travel or other special event——have been compared to directing a movie but is actually more like a (4)<u>live stage production</u>. It is a high—wire act without the safety nets. Once your event starts there are no (5) <u>second chance</u>. It's done in one take and there are no dress rehearsals. You are simply not able to (6)<u>predict the outcome</u> —as you can from a movie script— of how your guests and suppliers will (7) <u>interact and react</u>. But (8) <u>you can plan, prepare and then be prepared for the unexpected</u>. Any event, whether it's for 50 or more than 2,000, (9) <u>needs to be as detailed and as scripted as any film production</u>. Never forget Murphy's Law: (10) <u>what can go wrong, will go wrong</u>.

B. Multiple Choices

● Dialogue 1

Man: The sale of our new product was not so satisfactory last month.

Woma: Yes, so the board of directors has decided to hold a product launch this month.

Man: This is a go. Then how Many customers will be invited?

Woman: It's not set yet. It must depend on how much money will be set aside by the board.

Question 1. What's the purpose of the product launch?

Question 2. What should be decided before an event is put into practice according to the Dialogue?

● Dialogue 2

Man: Hey, you're in such a hurry! What's the problem?

Woman: The radio says that we're in for a storm tonight.

Man: So what?

Woman:	So I must hurry up to take care of the equipments and facilities in our exhibition halls.
Man:	I see. Let me give you a hand.Question 3. What is it that makes the Woman: go in a hurry?

Question 4. What can be inferred from the Dialogue?

• Dialogue 3

Man:	Hey, John, I was told that you've been promoted. Congratulations!
Woman:	Thanks, but the higher the position, the more duties.
Man:	Certainly. Then what're your responsibilities now?
Woman:	Event planning, say, I must Manage everything very well so the event can be a fun and success for every part.
Man:	That sounds a great job, but how can you Manage that?
Woman:	Firstly, I will have a talk with the sponsor of the event, consulting them about the goal and the budget of the event.
Man:	The first question you'd like to ask is "Should you hold an event?" or, "Do you have sufficient funds to stage an event?" Am I right?
Woman:	Exactly. And another two questions are: what's the purpose of the event? Does it justify the financial outlay?
Man:	But when planning major events, just thinking in terms of money will not make sense.
Woman:	You said it! A preliminary cost estimate and the event goal decision are the very starting-point, from which flow other necessities such as some internal factors, say, the targeted audience, the type of the event, Management and resources; and some external factors like the venue, timing, and transportation.
Man:	Besides, it's also of great necessity to set up an event committee or team seeking to match skills and areas of interest to areas of responsibility.
Woman:	Ah, sure. Bringing people together to work as a cooperative team and each member with a clearly-defined responsibility, this is the very foundation to ensure a successful event. It seems to me that you know the job quite well.
Man:	Thanks. Then do you think it is possible for me to be a member of your team?
Woman:	Aha, it will be our great pleasure!

Question5. What are the major responsibilities of an event-planning manager?

Question 6. What should be decided in the first place before an event is held?

Question 7. Which of the following may NOT necessarily be considered when an event is being planned?

Question 8. What requirements should an effective event team meet to ensure a successful event ?

● Dialogue 4

Man:	Several months ago a survey was conducted and the result shows that fairs and exhibitions have been considered the most efficient way to do business all in one shot.
Woman:	Really? What are the findings?
Man:	According to the survey, 51% of the attendees believe that exhibitions are the best marketing channels for demonstrating the benefits of the products and services; 37% claim exhibitions are the best channel for building relationships with the customers and prospects.
Woman:	So it seems that quite a large number of companies and Managers have been fully aware of the function of the events, meetings and exhibitions.
Man:	Yes. As a matter of fact, events and expositions have become one of the indispensable sections of business.
Woman:	But why do you think exhibitions and expos can have so much contribution to the business?
Man:	Mm... There are Many reasons why they can be so effective. Take a trade fair for example. There, the attendees are not only top-level buyers, but all the major players in the industry gathering in one place to compare exhibitors' products, and to get their questions answered fully and immediately.
Woman:	Then the role of the exhibition is self-evident.
Man:	And that's also why we can see a rapid Increase in the number of companies planning and participating in meetings and expos.
Woman:	But all meetings and expos cannot be great success, can they?
Man:	Certainly not. Instead, a meeting or exhibition can be spoiled by a lot of factors ranging from the cost estimate, timing, location and coordination to the transportation, logistics and weather.
Woman:	It's not an easy job to hold a successful event!

Man: Sure. But sInce we are sure of the bright future the MICE industry will enjoy, it's no reason for us not to do a fine job. Question 9. What questions are interviewees asked in the survey?

Question 10. What conclusion can be drawn from the survey?

Question 11. According to the Dialogue, why can a trade faire be effective for businesses?

Question 12. All meetings and exhibitions are not successful because_____.

Answers:

1. b; 2. d; 3. c; 4. a; 5. c; 6. b; 7. d; 8. c; 9. d; 10. d; 11. c; 12. b

C. Passage Dictation

To help make your Incentive trip, conference or exhibition a success, all you need to do is to discuss your requirements with our professionals. We'll draw on our expertise and resources to tailor a unique package for your group. Our conference and Incentive organizers aren't tied down to one way of doing things. They can solicit proposals from various suppliers, comparing cost and level of services to find what's best for you. Feel free to discuss ideas with them. Often the discussion process itself gives rise to new, exciting ideas for your objective. We are dedicated to providing top-level service, imaginative programs and value for money. We can assist your group in all aspects of the event, before, after and while your group is in Shanghai. Services offered by our company range from the destination management, complete meeting organizing, and planning and producing events to interpretation, translation services and coach and car hire. Donghai Convention Company, with its world-class facility and service, is right here waiting for you!

Section 2 Interpretation Activities

A. Sentence Interpretation

1. First, find out the equivalents of the following words.

1. retailer	
2. recreation facilities	
3. 獎勵旅遊	
4. 同義詞	
5. 區分	
6. 簡要介紹一下	
7. 無過多要求	

2. Read the following material to your partner; ask him or her to put them into Chinese or English.

1. Comparing both conventions, the biggest difference is size.
2. What's more, they look for attractive locations, recreation facilities, choice of restaurants, etc.
3. It was E. F. MacDonald who innovated the idea of Incentive travel.
4. One big advantage of exhibiting at this show is that we can meet retailers form all over the country.
5. By this design, you can easily find the show you want to visit.
6. 怎麼區分 "seminars" 和 "conventions" 呢？你認為它們是同義詞嗎？
7. 你說的不夠完整 '"congress" 在歐洲普遍使用，並用於國際會議。
8. 首先，讓我向你們簡要介紹一下我們中心。
9. 在諸多獎勵形式中，為何偏偏選種旅遊這種獎勵形式？
10. 我意思是說他們對會議設施並無過多要求。

B. Passage Interpretation

1. First, find out the equivalents of the following words.

1. overlap		5. 消費者展覽	
2. quantify		6. 分離出	
3. premise		7 贏取利潤	
4. 貿易展覽		8 同時進行	

2. Read the following passages and translate them into Chinese or English.

● **Passage 1**

Meetings, whether they are conferences or conventions, Increasingly overlap with Incentive travel. This is because companies both at home and abroad are attaching much importance to rewarding Good performance of employees.

Association meetings are staged where local associations are highly active. Many international associations, like the World Exposition Organization, choose a venue for practical reasons, Including the supporting interests.

While the meeting industry is concerned with communicating information, it is hard to quantify the different types of meetings involved. What makes up a meeting depend on the minimum number of attendees, the length of time, the subjects or activities and sometimes the type of premises.

Your Answer

_____

_____

_____

_____

_____

_____

_____

_____

● **Passage 2**

同協會會議一樣，展覽亦需要周密的計畫和組織, 這主要是因為展覽的籌備期較長、初期風險較大。一旦貿易展覽和消費者展覽組織成功，總是趨向于成為定期展覽，規模不斷壯大，從而分離出更多的專業展覽會。

展商可能有自己單獨的展台，或者聯合成為一個團體，他們時常提前預訂展位，以保證得到最好的位置。

與會議相比較而言，成功地組織的展覽通常能夠為展廳主和展覽會組織者贏取利潤。展覽和會議時常同時進行；大型的或者專業貿易展覽會一般在展覽期間穿插一些作為增加吸引力或發佈資訊的研討會，參展者可選擇性地參與其中。

Your Answer

_____

_____

_____

_____

_____

_____

_____

_____

_____

Reference Answers

A. Sentence Interpretation

1.

1. retailer	零售商
2. recreation facilities	康樂設施
3. 獎勵旅遊	Incentive travel/tour
4. 同義詞	synonym
5. 區分	distinguish
6. 簡要介紹一下	give a sketch of
7. 無過多要求	less demanding

2.

1. 比較起來，兩個會議的最大區別在於會議規模不相同。
2. 再者，他們需要的是迷人的景點、康樂設施、精選餐館等。
3. 正是 E. F. MacDonald 創立了獎勵旅遊的概念。
4. 參加這個展覽的一大優點在於能接觸到來自全國各地的零售商。

5. 這種設計的優點在於幫助你迅速找到你要參觀的展覽。

6. How do you distinguish seminars from conventions? Do you think they are synonyms?

7. And to complete your list, congress is most commonly used in Europe and in international events.

8. To start with, let me give you a brief sketch of our center.

9. Among all forms of rewards, why are people given Incentive travels?

10. What I mean is that they are less demanding for meeting facilities.

B. Passage Interpretation

1.

1. overlap 重疊	2. quantify 用數量表示
3. premise 房屋連地基	4. 貿易展覽 trade fair
5. 消費者展覽 consumer fair	6. 分離出 to hive off
7. 贏取利潤 to generate profits	8. 同時進行 to be held in parallel

2.

● **Passage 1**

　　會議，無論他們是一般會議或大會，正趨向與獎勵旅遊相結合。這是國內外公司都重視對職員的良好表現進行獎勵的結果。

　　協會會議總是在地方性的協會高度活躍的地方召開。許多國際協會，為了一個特定理由，包括當地民眾的支持力度，選擇一個舉辦位址。比如，上海，中國的最大城市，以其極大的熱情贏得 2010 年世界博覽會舉辦權。

　　會議用於傳遞資訊時，很難說有多少種不同種類的會議。構成會議的要素取決於出席者最少人數，會期的長短，主題或活動類型，以及所選會址類型。

● **Passage 2**

　　Like association meetings, exhibitions need careful planning and organization, involving long lead times and initially a high degree of risk. Once established, trade fairs and consumer exhibitions tend to continue to be held as a regular calendar event, invariably growing in size and hiving off more specialist exhibitions.

Individual exhibitors may occupy stands exclusively or join together as an associated group in a larger assembly, and often need to reserve space well ahead to secure prime positions.

Compared with meetings, established exhibitions usually generate operating profits both for the hall providers and organizers of the events. Exhibits and meetings are often held in parallel; large or specialized trade fairs commonly Include optional seminars as an additional attraction and related source of information.

Section 3 Speaking Activities

A. Specialized Terms

Match the expressions on the left with the best equivalent Chinese on the right.

1. event	A. 職業會議策劃者
2. sponsor	B. 會議中心
3. planner	C. 與會者
4. attendee	D. 主旨發言人
5. venue	E. 大型活動（會展、節慶等）
6. convention center	F. 目的地管理公司
7. keynoter	G. 贊助方
8. CVB (Convention and Visitors Bureau)	H. 會議觀光局
9. CMP (Certified Meeting Planner)	I. 會後旅遊
10. DMC (Destination Management Company)	J. 註冊會議策劃師
11. PCO (Professional Conference Organizer)	K. 會議策劃者
12. post-conference tour	L. 會展場地

B. Sample Conversation

Listen and read aloud.

Situation: A foreign planner calls the sales office of Shanghai Convention and Visitors Bureau. He asks various questions about holding an annual association conference in the city. The clerk at the reception desk is answering him by providing the information the caller enquires about.

(一位國外會議策劃者打電話到上海會議局。他就在該市舉辦一個行業年會問了許多問題。一位元接待員在電話裡一一作答。)

Clerk:	Shanghai Convention and Visitors Bureau. May I help you?
Planner:	Yes. I'm John Stevens, calling from New Orleans. We're planning to hold a conference in your city. So I was wondering if you could give me some relevant information.
Clerk:	It's a pleasure. What would you like to start with?
Planner:	Would you tell me if we could hold the conference at a hotel or at a convention center of the city?
Clerk:	It all depends. For how Many attendees?
Planner:	About 60 people.
Clerk:	Then I think a medium-sized meeting room will do. All hotels in the city each have conference centers offering such meeting rooms.
Planner:	Good. One more thing, what will the weather be like there in October?
Clerk:	In Shanghai, October is the most agreeable of the season, with clear sky casting golden sunshine, and gentle breeze blowing. The temperature is about 18—23°C , or 64.4—73.4 °F .
Planner:	Sounds wonderful. We plan to have a post-conference tour, and it seems we've chosen the right time. By the way, what can we expect to see there?
Clerk:	There are a Good variety of places worth sightseeing both in the city proper and the neighboring towns. For a shopping tour, you may go to Yu Yuan Garden. For a commanding view over the whole city, you may mount on to the Oriental Peal Tower. To meet your religious interest, the Jade Buddha Temple is the ideal place.
Planner:	You can certainly help us a lot with the tour, will you?
Clerk:	Sure, we can. We can also help you liaise a property to hold your conference once you've make a decision.
Planner:	Thank you very much for the information. We'll let you know our decision in a week's time.
Clerk:	Please feel free to contact us if you have any question in your mind.
Planner:	We will. Thanks again. Goodbye.
Clerk:	Goodbye. Thanks for calling.

C. Functional Expressions

Read aloud and practice with your partner.

1. How to elicit questions politely	Response
Can I help you?	Yes, I'd like to be told some general information about the city's meeting facilities.
May I help you?	Yes, we're planning a meeting.
How may I help you?	I want to know the dress code for attending the conference.
How may I assist you?	It's Su-Hui calling from China and we plan to hold a conference in UK.

2. How to make inquiries politely	Response
Excuses me, would you mind answering a few questions?	No, not at all.
Excuses me, I wonder if you'd mind answering a few questions?	Of course not.
Could you tell me what the weather is like there?	Yes, certainly.
Do you think you could tell me what the weather is like there?	Ok, I'll try.
I was wondering if you could tell me how to contact you?	You can either call us at 021-123456 or email us at cvb2010@hotmail.com.
May I ask how to contact you?	You can send us a fax to book the meeting.

3. How to verify information

Let me check. You said October. Is that right?

You did say 200 attendees, didn't you?

Forbes Global CEO Conference? Was it held in your place?

D. Speaking Up

Translate the following sentences into English by using as many language skills learnt as possible.

1. 肯勞得會議中心。有何吩咐？
2. 對不起先生, 打擾您了，我能知道您的姓名嗎？
3. 請問有多少人參加會議？
4. 請問貴城市有沒有天主教堂（Catholic Church）？
5. 你們飯店在接待會議方面有豐富的經驗，是這樣的嗎？

E. Role-play

Practise the conversations according to the situations.

● Situation 1

A major U.S. ABC Computer Corporation is calling the Shanghai Claude Hotel to get some information about the group prices of rooms and seasonal prices of rooms. In pairs, try the Dialogue using your real names. One person will be the assistant manager for ABC Computer Corporation. The other person will be the sales manager for the Shanghai Claude Hotel.

● Situation 2

You are a convention planner of Millipore Shanghai Office. You would like to get some information about holding a conference in Thompson Conference Center. You are calling Susan Zhu, sales clerk of Thompson Conference Center.

Information about you：

You are Joanna, a convention planner of Millipore Shanghai Office.

Intention: Hold a three-day annual sales meeting

Place: Thompson Conference Center

Time: Feb.14th ——Feb.16th, 2005

Number of attendees: 27

Room reservation:

3 presidential suites and 12 standard rooms for 3 nights

3 meeting rooms (1 for 10 people, 1 for 8 and the other for 9 on Feb. 15th and 16th

Activities during the meeting:

Holding an annual dinner on the night of Feb.14th, requirements:

A small dinning room with 3 tables

A toastmaster capable of both Chinese and English

The name lists on each table

Meeting room facilities:

1 overhead, 1 slide projectors and screen, booth draping tables, 1 podium, overhead projector pen

Questions the clerk might ask you:

    1. What types of hotel rooms are available in your Center?

    2. What types of meeting rooms are available in your Center?

    3. What types of meeting equipment do you offer in your Center?

    4. What tourist attractions will we expect to sightsee?

● **Situation 3**

You are Mary Zhu, a clerk of Convention Office. You are answering a phone call from a convention attendee who would like to get some information about it. Use the information below to answer the questions from the prospect.

Your card:

Information aabout you:

Room reservation: Hilton Hotel with a room rate of $100 per day

Jinjiang Hotel with a room rate of $120 per day

Jinjiang Hotel is nearer to the convention center.

Temperature: 18—23 ° C

Activities of post-conference tour:

- Sightseeing both in the city proper and the neighboring towns
- Shopping
- Mounting on to the Oriental Pearl Tower
- Jade Buddha Temple, etc.

Information you need to get from the other party:

Name of the caller?

Name of Convention?

Intention?

Room reservation?

Date?

The prospect's card:

Information about the prospect:

Shirley White: an attendee of the convention from U.S.

Convention: the 22nd World Nursing Congress, from May 24th to 28th

Intention: make sure the arrangement of the convention

Room reservation: Hilton Hotel with a room rate of $100 per day

jinjiang Hotel with a room rate of $120 per day

Date: from May 23rd to 28th

Questions the prospect might ask:

Wish to make sure of the arrangements of the congress?

Wish to reserve a room?

Climate of the city?

Temperature:Fahrenheit($F=C \times 1.8+32; C=F=(F-32)/1.8$)

Activities of post-conference tour?

Chapter 2
Booking an Event 招展商會展預訂

▌Section 1 Listening Activities

Learn these words and expressions before starting to listen to the tape.

top sales performance			傑出銷售業績
justify		v.	證明
client appreciation event			客戶聯誼活動
pique		v.	刺激
sales executive			銷售主管人員
initiative		n.	主動行動
motivation		n.	刺激
entail		v.	需要
contagious		A.	觸染性的
prospect		n.	可能性很大的潛在客戶
encounter		v.	遇見
convIncingly		adv.	使人信服地
crane		n.	起重機
return on investment			投資回報
enterprise		n.	企業
Shanghai Mart			上海世貿商城
conference delegate			會議代表

A. Spot Dictation

In the course of event planning, one of the most important things to consider is the goal or (1)_____ of the event. Why are you holding it? What are your goals and (2)_____? What do you hope to achieve? In any event, be clear about your (3)_____. It should be significant, such as (4)_____, say a new car, or rewarding (5)_____, to justify the cost of the event. And on the basis of (6)_____, the plan and the set-up of the event will be decided. For example, if you are planning a (7)_____ where

attendees at a conference may have several choices on the same evening, (8)_____
_____, get them to your event, (9)_____
_____. (10)_____
_____.

B. Multiple Choices

Directions: *In this section you will hear several Dialogues. After each Dialogue, there are some questions. Listen to the Dialogues carefully and choose the most appropriate answer to each question from the four choices marked A, B, C and D.*

● **Dialogue 1**

1. What does the company decide to launch?
   A. A meeting.
   B. A party.
   C. An Incentive program.
   D. A reception.

2. Why does the company decide to launch the program?
   A. Because it needs extra budget.
   B. Because it can help the staff relax themselves.
   C. Because it can help the manager to be promoted.
   D. Because it helps to motivate and inspire the staff members.

● **Dialogue 2**

3. Why is the event held by ABC Company thought of as a success?
   A. Because there are more attendees in the event than before.
   B. Because both the host and the guests benefit a lot from it.
   C. Because the host earns a lot of money from it.
   D. Because the guests earn a lot of money from it.

4. What can be inferred from the Dialogue?
   A. People and companies are involved in events with some certain purposes.
   B. Events can always profit the host and attendees.

C. More and more people are willing to attend an event.

D. In an event attendees can get to know customers.

• Dialogue 3

5. Why is it said that "business event industry becomes a sellers' market"?

A. Because the industry used to be dominated by buyers.

B. Because there are fewer and fewer buyers.

C. Because people are more interested in events than before.

D. Because more companies reenter the meetings and Incentive market.

6. What does "a sellers' market" imply according to the Dialogue?

A. Buyers will have more choices.

B. The competition among exhibition companies will be more severe

C. The quality of the event industry will be improved greatly.

D. The quality of the industry will be better.

7. What will be a possible solution to ensure the competence?

A. Deciding the target market and clarifying its expectations and objectives.

B. Improvement at the level of management.

C. Enlarging and broadening the target market.

D. Establishing rapports with clients.

8. Why is it necessary to make clear the objectives and expectations of the clients?

A. Because it will help to enlarge the market.

B. Because it will help to obtain the trust on the part of the clients.

C. Because it will help to decide the management and policies of the exhibition company.

D. Because clients are the gods of the company.

• Dialogue 4

9. What's the problem the company is faced up with?

A. The quality of its products decreased.

B. The sales of its products dropped.

C. It lost contact with its clients.

D. There are no new and effective policies.

10. In comparison with advertisement, what advantages will fairs and exhibitions have?

    A. Exhibitions are more economical.

    B. Exhibitions can attract more clients.

    C. Exhibitions can show and demonstrate products more directly and more convIncingly.

    D. Exhibitions can help more to improve the image of the company.

11. What prevents the company from participating in exhibitions and fairs?

    A. The high cost expected.

    B. The trouble to show a crane.

    C. The policies of the board.

    D. No one to give it professional suggestions and assistance.

12. According to the Dialogue, what are the goals of the company to participate in an exhibition?

    A. To find a new marketing practice to take the place of advertisements.

    B. To provide some new and effective advice for the board.

    C. To establish a kind of rapport with its clients.

    D. To Increase the sales on a relatively tight budget.

C. Passage Dictation

Directions: *In this section, you will hear a passage. Listen carefully and write down what you hear on the tape.*

_____

_____

_____

_____

_____

_____

_____

_____

_____

Tape script & Answers

A. Spot Dictation

Tape script:

In the course of event planning, one of the most important things to consider is the goal or (1) <u>purpose</u> of the event. Why are you holding it? What are your goals and (2) <u>intentions</u>? What do you hope to achieve? In any event, be clear about your (3) <u>objective</u>. It should be significant, such as (4) <u>launching a major product</u>, say a new car, or rewarding (5) <u>top sales performance</u>, to justify the cost of the event. And on the basis of (6) <u>the settled goal</u>, the plan and the set-up of the event will be decided. For example, if you are planning a (7) <u>client appreciation event</u> where attendees at a conference may have several choices on the same evening, (8) <u>your objective would be to create something that will pique their interest</u>, get them to your event, (9) <u>keep them there and have them interacting with your people</u>. (10) <u>Always bear in your mind your targeted audience and your objectives</u>.

B. Multiple Choices

Tape script:

• **Dialogue 1**

Man: Manager Wong, I was told that our company has decided to hold an Incentive program for the winning sales executives.

Woman: It's true. We believe that it will inspire the initiative and motivation of our staff members.

Man: But it will entail some extra budget.

Woman: So long as after it, the staff can work with a higher motivation and contagious enthusiasm.

• **Dialogue 2**

Man: I attended an event held by ABC Company last week.

Woman: Was it a success?

Man: Absolutely, for both the host and the attendees.

Woman:	For what?
Man:	The Company has learned more about its clients' and prospects' expectations; and I know more about my competitors.
Woman:	So that's why more and more people and companies would like to present themselves in events and exhibitions.

● Dialogue 3

Man:	John...John...John
Woman:	Ah, Yes? ...Sorry, I am too absorbed in this passage.
Man:	What is it?
Woman:	It's entitled "Business event industry becomes a sellers' market". You know what, it's said that this year will see a shift from years of the industry being dominated by the whims of buyers to that of a sellers' market, as more companies re-enter the meetings and Incentives market in the US and globally.
Man:	So what?
Woman:	It means our exhibition company will encounter more and more competitors.
Man:	Then we must do something to improve our competence.
Woman:	Exactly! The question is how.
Man:	Mm...According to a Chinese saying, we should "know our own situation and that of others". If we can make clear the goals and expectations of the clients and hereby perform our responsibilities and reveal our competence, perhaps the task will be easier for us.
Woman:	You said it! Therefore, the first thing we must do is to examine and survey our targeted market; then decide what is needed and what can be done to meet our clients' objectives.
Man:	But ours is a comprehensive exhibition company targeting a variety of event and exhibition markets, so it will be a big project to clarify the expectations and objectives of the clients.
Woman:	It is really painstaking but it is worthwhile in that it will help us decide our techniques and services, policies and Management.
Man:	We should always keep in mind our "Gods" and what they need and want to achieve.
Woman:	That's the point!

● Dialogue 4

Woman: Good morning, Mr. Hilton. Nice to meet you, is there anything I can do for you?

Man: Yes. You know, we met some problems in our sales these days. One major product of our company, the crane, its sales dropped a lot in the latest months. But we can assure that its quality is at the top level in the engineering field.

Woman: I see. That means you've lost some of your clients in the past months.

Man: Yes, exactly.

Woman: So you must try to improve your marketing policies and practice.

Man: We do produce some advertisements.

Woman: Mm...Compared with advertisements, perhaps participating in an exhibition will work more effectively in that exhibitions will allow you to demonstrate the technical quality of your products more convIncingly.

Man: In fact, we often receive various invitations asking us to attend meetings, exhibitions, fairs and something like that.

Woman: Then why don't you take them?

Man: Err...You know, it's not an easy job to demonstrate a crane in an exhibition.

Woman: I know it will be a big program, especially in terms of the cost. But I'll bet the cost can be justified.

Man: How come?

Woman: Indeed fairs and exhibitions are more than just a marketing tool; they will be your whole marketplace to a certain degree.

Man: Really?

Woman: Sure. As a matter of fact, they help you to win new customers, renew contacts with your past customers and entertain your existing and loyal customers.

Man: How about the cost? Will that entail a large budget?

Woman: Just the contrary. Fairs and exhibitions are the most cost-effective way to get directly to the heart of your business sector, in one place and at one time.

Man: So now I can put forward the suggestion to our board that attending a trade show or exhibition is a necessity indeed. It will help to generate our sales, and generate a high return on investment.

Woman: Let's move on!

Answers:

1. C; 2. D; 3. B; 4. A; 5. D; 6. B; 7. A; 8. C; 9. B; 10. C; 11. A; 12. D

C. Passage Dictation

Shanghai provides a stage for local multimedia enterprises as well as foreign enterprises who want to explore the Chinese market. Multimedia Shanghai 2004 was the first professional event with a core of multimedia technology to be hosted by Shanghai, and also the first one to specialize in multimedia expo demonstration for the multimedia digital sector in China. Multimedia Shanghai 2009 will be held at Shanghai Mart on September 26-28 2009, and will be supported by some authoritative organizations such as Shanghai World Expo (Group) Co. Ltd. (EXPO), and Chinese Association of Natural Science Museums (CANSM).

With a theme of "Multimedia with World Expo", Multimedia Shanghai 2009 will feature numerous technical seminars for the introduction of new multimedia products and technology from over 120 leading technology vendors and developers. It will provide the perfect forum to show new products to over 8,000 projected expo attendees and 450 conference delegates, Including top Government officials, leading local and international multimedia experts, and decision-makers from global enterprise markets.

Multimedia Shanghai 2009, the most anticipated multimedia technology event in Asia!

Section 2 Interpretation Activities

A. Sentence Interpretation

1. First, find out the equivalents of the following words.

1. innovation		6. 經裝修一新	
2. attendance		7. 音像設備	
3. distraction		8. 省去 …… 的麻煩	
4. keynoter		9. 滿足要求	
5. attendee		10. 會議套餐	

2. Read the following to your partner for him or her to put them down in Chinese or English.

1. I've heard so much about what your firm has been doing in the area of printer technology and application. And I'm eager to hear more about your innovation.

2. What is your average attendance at your annual convention?

3. Our meeting rooms are free from distraction so that the keynoters can make his/her speeches well understood.

4. The speaker is able to control lights, sound and projection from a single station because each meeting room has built-in audio and visual aids with individual control stations in each possible subdivision of the space.

5. Your center may not be as attractive to our attendees as the new resort in your area.

6. 我瞭解到你認為我們的中心不夠現代化。但是，我們的客房和會議室已經裝修一新，擁有全套在本地區頗具競爭力的設施。

7. 我們這裡的音像設備將極大地促進你們的培訓會議，難道您不這樣認為嗎？

8. 我們提供 24 小時會議室服務，這樣就能夠省去每天會議結束後搬運培訓材料的麻煩，同時也無需在第二天重新安裝設備。

9. 我認為我們的專案能夠滿足你們的要求。我們找個時間一起吃頓午飯並討論一下貴方的培訓會議，您以下如何？

10. 有關我們的中心和我們近期為本地企業度身定做的會議套餐，我想您一定會感興趣的。

B. Passage Interpretation

1. First, find out the equivalents of the following words.

1. double occupancy		6. 抵店	
2. brochure		7. 離店	
3. fact sheet		8. 提前報到者	
4. accolade		9. 出行安排	
5. 無需說		10. 住宿服務	

2. Read the following passages to yourself and render them into Chinese or English.

● **Passage 1**

We have already established our convention rates for this year. Currently, our Group Plan No.1 during August are RMB 700 yuan single and RMB 750 yuan double occupancy. Group Plan No. 2 Includes room, breakfast/lunch/dinner and is currently RMB 1,200 yuan single and RMB 1,400 yuan double occupancy. I've enclosed several descriptive brochures along with a most comprehensive fact sheet. As you can see, we do make available this area's most complete convention hotel. We are the only hotel in our area that has its own 18-hole championship course and a tennis center. Also, please keep in mind that we are a five-star hotel. We've maintained this accolade for the past 10 years.

Your Answer

_____

_____

_____

_____

_____

_____

_____

_____

● **Passage 2**

週二我們通過電話，我感到我們的交談很愉快。無需說，對於能夠有機會在八月份為貴協會服務，我們感到非常滿意。我們將在以下時間為你們提供十分舒適的的住宿服務：抵店時間—8 月 18 日，離店時間—8 月 22 日。 我們能夠接待 8 月 17 日（星期二）的提前報到者，人數限於 30 以下。如果你可以接受我在這裡列出的安排，請書面告知。我將為您初步預留一些會議室，這樣，這些會議室就不會被租借給其他會議主辦方。再次向您表示感謝。請告知您的出行安排，以便我能留出時間陪同您參觀我們肯勞得會議中心。

Your Answer

_____

_____

_____

_____

_____

_____

_____

_____

Reference Answers

A. Sentence Interpretation

1.

1. innovation	創新	6. 經裝修一新	completely renovated
2. attendance	參加會議的人數	7. 音像設備	audiovisual equipment
3. distraction	干擾物	8. 省去 …… 的麻煩	Save the trouble
4. keynoter	主旨發言人	9. 滿足要求	Meet one's demand
5. attendee	與會者	10. 會議套餐	Meeting package

2.

1. 對於貴公司在印表機技術和應用領域的長期努力，我知之甚多。我非常想瞭解更多的有關你們的創新故事。

2. 你們參加年會的人數平均是多少？

3. 我們的會議室沒有干擾物（噪音），主旨發言人的講話能夠聽得很清楚。

4. 發言人在同一個地方就可以控制燈光、聲音和投影儀，這是因為每個會議室都有內置的聲像輔助設備，並且各自都有相對獨立的控制台。

5. 比起你們的新度假勝地，貴中心對我們的與會者並不具有同樣的吸引力。

6. I learn that you don't feel our center is modern enough. But our rooms and meeting space have been completely renovated and offer all competitive amenities found in our area.

7. Don't you think our audiovisual equipment will greatly enhance your training sessions?

8. We offer 24-hour meeting room service, so that it can eliminate the trouble of removing training materials each evening and resetting equipment the next morning.

9. I think our program can best meet your demand. When could we meet for lunch to discuss your training sessions?

10. I though you'd be interested in hearing about our center and the meeting package we have just designed for local businesses.

B. Passage Interpretation

1.

1. double occupancy	入住雙人房	6. 抵店	arrival
2. brochure	小冊子	7. 離店	departure
3. fact sheet	情況說明	8. 提前報到者	early arrival
4. accolade	榮譽	9. 出行安排	travel arrangement
5. 無需說	needless to say	10. 住宿服務	accommodation service

2.

● Passage 1

我們已經制定了今年的會議價格。目前，八月份的一號團隊價格分別為單人房每夜間人民幣 700 元，雙人房每夜間人民幣 750 元。二號團隊價格為單人房每夜間人民幣 1,200 元，雙人房每夜間人民幣 1,400 元，包括客房、早餐 / 午餐 / 晚餐。隨信附寄幾份介紹小冊子以及一份詳細的情況說明書。正如您看到的那樣，我們是本地設施齊全的飯店。當地只有我們這家飯店有 18 洞冠軍賽高爾夫球場和一個網球場。同時，請您記住我們是一家五星級飯店，我們保持著這個殊榮已有十餘載。

● Passage 2

Certainly enjoyed our telephone conversation on Thursday, and needless to say, we are gratified at the prospect of serving your association in August. We could very comfortably accommodate you for arrival Wednesday, August 18 with departure Sunday, August 22. We could accept some early arrivals on Tuesday, August 17. However, it would be limited to 30 guest rooms. If the arrangements I outlined are agreeable, please drop me a note and I will protect some meeting space for you on a tentative basis so that the space does not disappear to another meeting planner. Thank you again, and please let me know about your travel arrangements so that I can set aide the necessary time to personally acquaint you with the Claude.

Section 3 Speaking Activities

A. Specialized Terms

Match the expressions on the left with the best Chinese equivalent on the right.

1. MICE (meeting, Incentive tour, conference, exhibition)	A. 專家討論會
2. convention	B. 專業會議
3. conference	C. 產品發佈會
4. plenary session	D. 會展（總稱）
5. seminar	e. 流程實習
6. workshop	f. 懂事會議，全體成員會議
7. product launch;	g. 協會年會
8. board meeting	h. 研討會
9. fund-raiser	i. 募捐會
10. forum	j. 論壇
11. panel	k. 培訓會議
12. training session	l. 全體會議

B. Sample Conversation

Listen and read aloud.

Situation: Jiang Lin, director of convention sales department of Claude Convention Center, is meeting Mr. Rachel, the meeting planner, to discuss holding a meeting at the property.

肯勞得會議中心銷售部主任江林，他正在和會議主辦方 Rachel 先生就在該中心舉辦一次會議進行商談。

Director: Glad to meet you, Mr. Rachel. I'm Jiang Lin, director of convention sales department.

Mr.Rache: The pleasure is mine. I'm here to discuss with you about holding a meeting at your property.

Director:	Happy to be of any help to you. What meeting is it?
Mr.Rache:	An annual convention of the Translators Association. The attendees are top translators across the world.
Director:	Can I see the name list of the attendees?
Mr.Rache:	Certainly. Here it is.
Director:	Oh, I see. There are 100 attendees. I think our medium-sized meeting room can serve the purpose.
Mr.Rache:	Do you have sufficient number of breakout rooms? We have several seminars after the plenary session.
Director:	At this time of high season, we'll use public space if necessary. Here are the convention brochures showing the details about meeting facilities.
Mr.Rache:	Thank you. I shall consult with the president of the association. We'll let you know by fax once we've decided.
Director:	Thank you for coming. We look forward to seeing you soon again.

C. Functional Expressions

Read aloud and practice with your partner.

Introducing the capacity and capability of the convention center

Here is the rental rate list for equipment and personnel for the convention.

We have some brand new imported equipment.

It accommodates about 400 people.

Our conference hall is multi-purpose.

We have a fully-equipped convention center that provides complete secretarial service.

We have all the state-of-art audiovisual equipment.

Giving further information about meeting booking

You can hire our nightclub for private use.

I will send you a support facilities list with a price list by fax.

So you'd like to reserve our conference room for 3 days together with an overhead projector.

I'll order a complete range of pens in different colors.

D. Speaking Up

Render the following into English by using as many language skills learnt as possible.

1. 這個多功能廳中心是主會議禮堂，能容納 400 人。

2. 這是我們的會議服務指南，裡面有關於會前、會中和會後服務的詳盡描述。

3. 能有這個機會為你們服務，我們感到十分榮幸。今天，我們能否從確定會議日期談起呢？

4. 該設備音像品質具佳。

5. 除免費房間外，會議工作人員還可以享用優惠價格房。

E. Role-play

Practise the conversations acoording to the situations.

• **Situation 1**

You are a clerk with the local convention and visitors bureau (CVB). You are talking with a prospective customer on the phone, to arrange a fam trip to Qingpu, Shanghai. You explain the tour schedule to the caller.

You should say or explain:

The duration of the fam. Tour.

What is Included (meals, transportation, etc.) and how are they arranged.

Whom the invitation Includes (spouse, other members of the selection committee, etc.).

The tour program: a. A camping to one of the best local destinations; b. Experience in the hotels, museums, restaurants and places of scenery and interes.

• **Situation 2**

You are the Auto Expo project manager of the Galaxy Exhibition Company. You are planning an exhibition. You are visiting Mr. Li Ming with the local exhibition center. You discuss /negotiate the price terms for reserving exhibition space with Mr. Li Ming.

You should ask these questions:

Capacity of the center?

Price scale?

Counter offer?

Lower price?

Discount?

Wish to extend the closing hour of the day?

Reference Answers

D. Speaking Up

1. The center of the multi-purpose hall is the main conference auditorium seating 400.

2. This is our meeting prospectus, containing a complete description about services before, during and after meetings.

3. It's an honor to have this opportunity of serving your. Today, shall talk about the date of meeting, to begin with?

4. The equipment is of Good quality of both picture and sound.

5. Meeting staff can be offered rooms with a discounted room rate as well as complimentary rooms.

Chapter 3
Event Planning and Budgeting 會展策劃與預算

▌Section 1 Listening Activities

Go over the following words and expressions before listening to the tape.

1 negotiation		n.	商議 , 談判
2 refund		n.	退款
3 package		n.	由好幾項內容構成的建議
4 preposition		n.	預先定位或放置
5 brand awareness	品牌認知度		

A. Spot Dictation

　　(1)_____ may seem to someone a simple matter of asking a rich company for money and the money may be treated as a (2)_____. However, sponsorship is never a donation. It is a (3)_____ technique used by businesses, whether large or small, for merely (4)_____ ___. It is commercial because the sponsor believes the event will offer a more (5)_____ _____ to the targeted market. Sponsors not only provide money, services or other support to MICE events, but (6) _____ _____ _____. These benefits may (7)_____ _____ _____ _____. To ensure these benefits are given to the sponsor requires the event management time, planning and effort. (8)_____ _____ _____.

B. Multiple Choices

Directions: *In this section you will hear several Dialogues. After each Dialogue, there are some questions. Listen to the Dialogues carefully and choose the most appropriate answer to each question from the four choices marked A, B, C and D.*

● **Dialogue 1**

1. Why is Chen Hua calling Mr. Jacobs?

   A. To get his sponsorship for an international conference on MICE education.

   B. To have a business negotiation with him.

   C. To sell exhibition products to him.

   D. None of the above.

2. What will the event offer to Mr. Jacobs if he sponsors the event?

   A. It offers a research project to him.

   B. It may help him develop a strategy for marketing meeting facilities.

   C. It offers an opportunity to him to show his meeting product capabilities.

   D. It offers opportunity to him to buy meeting facilities.

3. Why does Chen Hua ask for Mr. Jacobs address?

   A. To meet him in person.

   B. To send him a sponsorship proposal.

   C. To discuss details with him in person.

   D. To write him a letter.

● **Dialogue 2.**

4. What do you know about Mr. Lee's exhibition and conference company?

   A. A world famous exhibition and conference organizer.

   B. A leading exhibition and conference organizer in the country.

   C. An ordinary local exhibition and conference organizer in the country.

   D. Not given.

5. What do you learn about the previously held Auto Sourcing exhibitions?

   A. They had only a few exhibitors.

   B. They had only a few visitors.

C. They had only Chinese exhibitors.

D. Only a few foreign companies signed up for these exhibitions.

6. How many months should there be between two exhibitions of the same kind?

    A. One month.

    B. Two months.

    C. One year.

    D. Half a year.

● Dialogue 3.

7. Which of the following statements about the renting of raw space is true?

    A. Each exhibitor is allowed to rent only twenty-seven square meters.

    B. One square meter of raw spaces costs RMB 2,050 yuan.

    C. Raw space costs at least RMB 24,550 yuan per square meter.

    D. The maximum area for one indoor raw space is twenty-seven square meters.

8. How large is each package stand?

    A. Nine square meters.

    B. Twenty-seven square meters.

    C. Ninety square meters.

    D. Nineteen square meters.

● Dialogue 4.

9. Which booth is reserved for the exhibitor?

    A. Booth GO72.

    B. Booth GR72.

    C. Booth CR17.

    D. Booth CO27.

10. What will the exhibitor do to cancel the space reservation?

    A. Submit a written notice prior to the event.

    B. Making a telephone call to the exhibition company.

    C. Mailing a 40% refund to the exhibition organizer.

    D. Writing a notice after the event.

C. Passage Dictation

Directions: *In this section, you will hear a passage. Listen carefully and write down what you hear on the tape.*

_____

_____

_____

_____

_____

_____

_____

_____

_____

Tape script & Answers:

A. Spot Dictation

Tape script:

(1) <u>Sponsorship</u> may seem to someone a simple matter of asking a rich company for money and the money may be treated as a (2) <u>donation</u>. However, sponsorship is never a donation. It is a (3) <u>promotional</u> technique used by businesses, whether large or small, for merely (4) <u>commercial reasons</u>. It is commercial because the sponsor believes the event will offer a more (5) <u>effective communication link</u> to the targeted market. Sponsors not only provide money, services or other support to MICE events, but (6) <u>they also look for intangible benefit in return for their sponsorship</u>. These benefits may (7) <u>Include creating consumer Goodwill towards the company, Increasing the sales of their products, Increasing</u> brand awareness, demonstrating product capabilities, identifying niche markets, etc. To ensure these benefits are given to the sponsor

requires the event management time, planning and effort. (8) <u>A sponsorship policy sets out the event planner's promises to attract and deliver sponsorship benefits.</u>

B. Multiple Choices

Tape script:

• Dialogue 1

Man:	Hello, may I know who's calling?
Woman:	Hello, Mr. Jacobs. My name is Chen Hua, sales Manager of the Rainbow Convention center.
Man:	What I can do for you?
Woman:	We're hosting an international conference on MICE education. I thought you would be interested in sponsoring this event.
Man:	Why should I? What will the event offer to me?
Woman:	I know from our research that you are developing a strategy for marketing meeting facilities. It is an opportunity to demonstrate product capabilities, isn't it?
Man:	Yes, perhaps. We will give it a consideration.
Woman:	Thanks for your concern. May I know your address, Mr. Jacobs? I will send you a sponsorship proposal.
Man:	That's Good. My address is 550, Wuzhong Road, Shanghai, 201103.
Woman:	Thank you. If you have any special needs, please note them down on the proposal. We look forward to a meeting to discuss details in person. See you then, Mr. Jacobs.
Man:	Goodbye.

• Dialogue 2

Man: 1:	Hi, Mr. Yang. Nice to see you again.
Man: 2:	Nice to see you, too, Mr. Lee. I've come to discuss with you some further details about China Auto Scouring Expo. 2005.
Man: 1:	We really appreciate the opportunity to host the Expo. As you know, we're a top-notch conference and exhibition organizer.
Man: 2:	That is why we choose your company as our organizer. We trust your ability.

Man: 1: Thanks. Well, to start with, what are the guidelines of the Expo?

Man: 2: You know, previously there were Auto Sourcing exhibitions, but only a few major foreign-funded manufacturers in China took part in them. We hope the 2005 Expo can attract more manufacturers both at home and from abroad.

Man: 1: I see what you mean. You want it to be an international Auto Expo in its real sense.

Man: 2: That's it. We are expecting 100 leading foreign companies from abroad and 600 major demotic auto companies.

Man: 1: In that case, we need to find a large exhibition center.

Man: 2: And when do you plan to hold the Expo?

Man: 1: It'll be subject to the changing market. We shall conduct a survey to find out if there will be exhibitions of the similar kind. You know, there must be an interval of 3-6 months. As for the exact dates, we'll do our best to give you a reply as soon as possible.

Man: 2: As a final point, we will sponsor you with a considerable amount of money. Further information about terms and conditions are stated in the draft contract.

Man: 1: It seems we have covered the major points for today?

Man: 2: Yes. When can we sign the agency agreement?

Man: 1: Humm, we have to give a serious consideration to the contract. Will tomorrow be all right?

Man: 2: OK with me. See you then.

Man: 1: Goodbye.

● **Dialogue 3**

Man: Grand Exhibition Company Limited. This is Santos. How may I help you?

Woman: Yes. I'd like to reserve a space at the International Art Fair. But can you explain to me the options of stands first?

Man: Sure. We offer package stand and raw space. The former is nine square meters each.

Woman: What is the area for raw space?

Man: The minimum area for one raw space indoor is twenty-seven square meters.

Woman: How much do you charge for the stands and raw space respectively?

Man: The package stands cost at least RMB 24,550 yuan per unit, equivalent to about 3,00 US dollars. And RMB 2,050 yuan per square meter for raw spaces, equivalent to 250 US dollars.

Woman: I know. You mean there are different costs for the package stands?

Man: Yes. Costs vary with the different locations of the stand.

Woman: What if I would choose the center one?

Man: It costs RMB 28,000 yuan per unit.

Woman: Okay. I'll take one.

•Dialogue 4

Man: Good morning. Global Exhibition. How may I assist you?

Woman: I've made a reservation for the Handicrafts Exhibition six months ago. There is no way I can come. What shall I do to cancel my registration?

Man: We will see what we can do. May I have your name, please?

Woman: I'm John Smith with American Andrew Art Gallery China Office.

Man: Let me have a check, please...

Yes, you've reserved a center booth on the first floor, and the booth number is GO72. Am I correct?

Woman: You're absolutely right.

Man: There are a few more things I need to clarify. We won't accept your cancellation unless you send us a written notice by the end of this month. And then you may receive a 40% refund from us.

Woman: I want to get a refund.

Man: You may receive a 40% refund from us.

Woman: Well, that's better than nothing. When can you mail the refund to me?

Man: According to the company's regulation, I'll mail the cancellation refund to you when the show is over. I hope you understand.

Woman: That's understood. Thank you. Goodbye.

Man: We look forward to your participation in our next show.

Answers:

A; 2. C; 3. B; 4. B; 5. D; 6. D; 7. B; 8. A; 9. A; 10. A

C. Passage Dictation

Tape script:

Once the sponsors are identified, the next step is to work out a sponsorship package that can satisfy both the sponsors' needs and the objectives of the event. Based on the research into the sponsors' needs, the package is launched at a competitive price. For example, if the cost to reach a similar target market using television is RMB 200 000, a sponsorship price of RMB 150 000 may be viewed as an attractive proposition by a company.

Finally, the potential sponsor is contacted and given a formal written proposal which Includes all the sponsor's special requirements. After about five days, this can be followed up by a telephone call to ask for a meeting to present the proposal in person. Once the sponsor has been found, a sponsorship business plan outlining both parties' responsibilities should be drawn up.

▌Section 2 Interpretation Activities

A. Sentence Interpretation

1. First, find out the equivalents of the following words.

1 stay within the budget		6 一般管理費用	
2 loss leader		7 固定費用	
3 admission fee		8 可變費用	
4 profit-oriented event		9 收支平衡	
5 draft budget		10 淨利潤	

2. Read the following to your partner for him or her to put them down in Chinese or English.

1. The best financial history is that which occurs over a three-year period. In some cases it is not possible to construct a precise history and the event manager must rely upon what is known at the time the budget is prepared or on estimates.

2. Once you have prepared a draft budget, seek the counsel of the accountant to review your budget and help you with establishing the various line items and account codes.

3. Producing a fair net profit is both challenging and possible for event management business. The challenge is that event managers must work with a wide range of clients and it is difficult to budget for each event carefully to ensure a net profit.

4. SInce the invention of the spreadsheet program for computers, accounting has never been the same. Commercial software package such as Quicken have allowed small businesspeople to record their journal entries quickly, accurately, and cost-effectively.

5. 會展活動的固定間接費用是指可預測的費用項目。例如租金、工資、保險費、電話費、以及支援活動管理正常運轉所需要的其他費用。

6. 一次會展活動，其固定費用的多寡並不取決於參加者人數的多少。比方說，租金就是一項固定費用。無論參加者人數是增加還是稍有減少，租金費用一般不會有什麼變動。

7. 可變費用的預測更加困難，原因是這些用品經常到最後時刻才購進，而且價格的波動較大。由於客戶經常到最後一分鐘才註冊，而且在許多會展活動中有越來越多的參加者臨時報名，因此，等到最後時刻才訂購用品是一件極其棘手的事情。

8. 創造可觀的利潤是會展經理的天然職責。淨利潤和毛利潤之間的差額，就是我們為組織會展活動而提供的固定間接費用資料。

B. Passage Interpretation

1. First, find out the equivalents of the following words.

budget preparatin	
estimate	
assumption	
邏輯思維方式	
捲入法律糾紛	

2. Read the following passages to yourself and render them into Chinese or English.

● Passage 1

The budget represents an action plan that each successful event manager must carefully develop. Budget preparation is probably the most challenging part in financial management sInce the entire preparation is usually based on limited information or assumptions. To complete the budget preparation, you should come up with estimates based on assumptions.

Your Answer

_____

_____

_____

_____

_____

_____

_____

_____

_____

● **Passage 2**

據說活動管理者是用右腦思考的，常常會忽視重要的邏輯思維方式，而這種思維方式有助於確保活動能夠長期成功。忽視財務問題很容易破壞一個有創意、成功的活動，並損害管理者的聲譽，捲入法律糾紛。

Your Answer

_____

_____

_____

_____

_____

_____

_____

_____

_____

Reference Answers

A. Sentence Interpretation

1.

1 stay within the budget	控制預算	6 一般管理費用	overhead expense
2 loss leader	虧本求購商品	7 固定費用	fixed expense
3 admission fee	入會費	8 可變費用	variable expense
4 profit-oriented event	利潤導向型活動	9 收支平衡	break even
5 draft budget	預算草案	10 淨利潤	net profit

2.

1. 財務歷史最好以三年的財務狀況為一個期限。如果出現無法準確構建一個財務歷史的情況時，會展經理人只有依靠在編制預算或進行預測時所掌握的情況編制預算。

2. 預算草案編制好之後，應當請會計師提出對預算編制的意見並說明設置各種明細科目和制定會計編號。

3. 對於會展管理公司而言，創造可觀的淨利潤既是一種挑戰，也是一種可能。所謂挑戰指的是，由於會展經理人接待的客戶範圍很廣，因此很難做到為所有的會展活動都編制出保證創造利潤的預算方案。

4. 在電腦試算表程式發明的助益下，會計職業的面貌已經煥然一新。像 Quicken 這樣的商務軟體包可以使小型企業快速、準確和經濟地註冊自己的日記帳。

5. Fixed overhead expenses of an organization are those predictable items such as rent, salaries, insurance, telephone, and other standard operating expenses required to support the event management business.

6. Fixed expenses of an individual event do not depend on the number of participants. For example, rent is a fixed expense. Rent expense usually does not vary when the number of participants Increases or decreases slightly.

7. Variable expenses are more difficult to predict because often they are purchased last minute from vendors and the prices may fluctuate. Due to last minute registrations and an Increase in walkup guests for a variety of events, it is extremely difficult to wait until the last minute to order certain items.

8. Event managers endeavor to produce a fair net profit. The difference between net profit and gross profit is the percentage of fixed overhead expenses that was dedicated to producing a specific event.

B. Passage Interpretation

1.

budget preparatin	編制預算
estimate	估算
assumption	假設
邏輯思維方式	logical thinking abilities
捲入法律糾紛	produce legal implications

2.

 **Passage 1**

　　預算是每一個成功的活動管理者都必須仔細制訂的行動計畫。由於預算制訂的整個過程都是建立在有限資訊和假設的基礎上，因此，它也許是財務管理工作中最具有挑戰性的部分。為完成預算的制訂工作，你應該在假設的基礎上作出一些預測。

● **Passage 2**

　　It is said that event managers depend on the right side of the brain and often ignore the important logical thinking abilities that help ensure long-term success. Financial ignorance can easily wreck a creative, successful event management business and destroy one's reputation as well as produce serious legal implications.

Section 3 Speaking Activities

A. Specialized Terms

Match the expressions on the left with the best Chinese equivalent on the right.

1. payment schedule	A. 可歸還的
2. balance	B. 現金記帳法
3. full amount	C. 支付期限
4. unit price	D. 單價
5. deposit for calls	e. 桌面展示
6. refundable	f. 展台展示
7. table top exhibit	g. 足額

8. area exhibit	h. 電話押金
9. booth exhibit	i. 可供預訂的展台類型
10. options	j. 大型器材地面展示
11. exhibit assignments	k. 餘額
12. cash accounting	l. 展位分配

B. Sample Conversation

Listen and read aloud.

Situation: Mr. Ding are talking about planning China Toy Expositin with Mrs. Li.

Woman: Good morning, Mr. Ding. Nice to see you again.

Man: Good morning. Mrs. Li. Glad to meet you again too. I've come here to talk with you some details about China Toy Exposition.

Woman: It's a pleasure. What would you like to start with?

Man: Well, I think it's our wish that China Toy Exposition will be an international expo and attract toy manufacturers both at home and from abroad.

Woman: How Many exhibitors are you expecting to attend this expo?

Man: We are expecting 200 leading foreign companies and 400 major domestic companies.

Woman: In that case, a large exhibition center is necessary.

Man: Sure. One more thing, we don't want to hold it in September. You know, another two toy exhibitions will be staged in Beijing and Hangzhou at that time.

Clerk: I quite agree with you. There should be an interval of 3-6 moths between similar exhibitions. We prefer April, 2007.

Planner: It seems to be a Good time.

Clerk: By the way, what is your budget for the expo? Have you set aside some money for marketing?

Planner: Actually, we haven't finished budget preparation. To some degree, we want to make a decision after you have completed the draft expo plan. In terms of budget for marketing, we will take it into consideration.

Clerk: Yes, we are sure to complete the plan as soon as possible.

Planner: Thank you very much. It seems we have covered major points today?

Clerk: Yes, and thank you again for choosing our company as the expo organizer.

| Planner: | Not at all, we really trust you. Goodbye. |
| Clerk: | Goodbye. |

C. Functional Expressions

Read aloud and practice with your partner.

Discussing plans	Response
What are your plans for exhibitions next year?	We are planning 2 international expos.
What do you have in your mind to plan an exhibition?	I have no idea.
Do you know what it signifies?	It does show the unique character of Shanghai.
I think there should be an interval of 3-6 months between two similar exhibitions.	I cannot agree with you more.

D. Speaking Up

Render the following into English by using as many language skills learnt as possible.

1. 這個展覽每年舉辦一次。
2. 我們公司是有多年組展經驗的組展企業。
3. 請問你們最近的展覽計畫是什麼？
4. 請問你們在展覽行銷方面的預算是多少？
5. 如果你願意的話，我可以給你介紹一下這個展覽。

E. Role-play

Practise the conversations according to the situations.

● **Situation 1**

Mr. Smith is searching a place to hold an exhibition in Chins, s home appliances company. He is talking with Mrs. Ding, a sales manager from a venue-searching agency, to get some information about o suitable place to stage the show.

• Situation 2

Two persons are talking about planning an international exhibition(theme, guideline, time, location, expected participants, etc.). Please try the Dialogue using your real names in pairs.

• Situation 3

The Rainbow Exhibition Service is planning an air conditioner show which is expecting 500 exhibitors. Each exhibitor needs a standard booth(3m3m). Decide how much space you have to reserve from the exhibition center, and negotiate the price with the center. Please try the Dialogue using your real names in pairs.

• Situation 4

Rose Li is working for an exhibition organizing company. Now she is answering a phone call from Henry Smith who is from the organizing committee of a tradeshow.

Reference Answers

A. Specialized Terms

1.C 2. K 3. G 4. D 5. H 6. A 7. E 8. J 9.I 10. B

D. Speaking Up

1. The show is held annually.
2. Our company is an exhibition organizer with many years of experience in organizing exhibitions.
3. What are your plans for exhibitions recently?
4. What is your budget for exhibition marketing?
5. I can brief you on the exhibition if you like.

Chapter 4
Providing Exhibit Information 提供展覽資訊

▌Section 1 Listening Activities

Go over the following words and expressions before listening to the tape.

1 tantamount		a.	等價
2 astounding		a.	令人驚駭的
3 meteoric		a.	流星的，輝煌而短暫的
4 proprietary		a.	所有的，私人擁有的
5 down payment			預付定金
6. megaevents			超大型會展、節慶、賽事活動

A. Spot Dictation

You may have the (1)_____ event product, but unless you have a strategic plan for promoting this product, it will remain the best kept (2)_____ in the world. Even large, well-known (3)_____ such as the Super Bowl, Rose Parade, and Olympic Games require well-developed promotion strategies to (4)_____ they require.

The promotion strategy you identify for your event requires a careful study of past or (5)_____, expert guidance from people who have (6)_____ in this field, and most important, (7)_____ for specific measurement of your individual promotion activities.

(8)_____. First, you may measure awareness by your target market. (9)_____
_____. Next, you may measure actual attendance and the resulting investment. (10)_
_____. Did the promotions you designed persuade the participants or guests to attend the event?

B. Multiple Choices

Directions: *In this section you will hear several Dialogues. After each Dialogue, there are some questions. Listen to the Dialogues carefully and choose the most appropriate answer to each question from the four choices marked A, B, C and D.*

● **Dialogue 1**

1. Which one of the following belongs to the indoor advertisement?

   A. Indoor TV screens.

   B. Billboards.

   C. Color flags.

   D. Balloon advertisements.

2. What is the main advantage of indoor booth billboard according to the Dialogue?

   A. It is very interesting.

   B. It has Good effect.

   C. It help customers find the booth quickly.

   D. It has a reasonable price.

3. What kind of advertisement does the exhibitor decide to choose at last?

   A. Indoor TV screens.

   B. Not mentioned.

   C. Indoor booth billboard.

   D. Indoor advertising.

● **Dialogue 2**

4 What can not be rented at the information desk in the exhibition hall?

   A. Lanterns.

   B. Desks.

   C. Plants.

   D. Show boxes.

5. Which one of the following doesn't the exhibitor need?

   A. Show box.

   B. Lights.

C. Flowers.

D. Plants.

6. Where should the exhibitor settle the accounts?

    A. At the information desk.

    B. At the reception desk.

    C. At Window 2.

    D. At the office f the exhibition hall.

● **Dialogue 3.**

7. How many times has Miss Li's company taken part in this exhibition?

    A. Once.

    B. Never.

    C. Three times.

    D. Twice.

8. How much does Miss Li's company most probably pay for the standard booth?

    A. More than 4500 Yuan.

    B. Less than 500 Yuan.

    C. Less than 4500 Yuan if they choose the booth on the upper floor.

    D. Less than 4500 Yuan.

9. What is the meaning of "down payment" in the Dialogue?

    A. All needed payment.

    B. Half of the needed payment.

    C. Deposit for the booth.

    D. Fee for the booth.

● **Dialogue 4.**

10. What kind of textiles does the visitor pay more attention to?

    A. Silk textiles.

    B. Linen textiles.

    C. Cotton textiles.

    D. Viscose (纖維膠) textiles.

11. What does the pattern on cheongsams symbolize?

A. Tradition.

B. Luck.

C. Longevity.

D. Wealth.

12. What does the visitor seem to be most interested in?

A. Gowns.

B. Chinese "qipao".

C. Pajamas.

D. Shirts.

C. Passage Dictation

Directions: *In this section, you will hear a passage. Listen carefully and write down what you hear on the tape.*

_____

_____

_____

_____

_____

_____

_____

_____

_____

Tape script & Answers

A. Spot Dictation

You may have the (1) best-quality event product, but unless you have a strategic plan for promoting this product, it will remain the best kept (2) secret in the world. Even large, well-known (3) megaevents such as the Super Bowl, Rose Parade, and

Olympic Games require well-developed promotion strategies to (4) <u>achieve</u> they require.

The promotion strategy you identify for your event requires a careful study of past or (5) <u>comparable efforts</u>, expert guidance from people who have (6) <u>specific expertise</u> in this field, and most important, (7) <u>setting benchmarks</u> for specific measurement of your individual promotion activities.

(8) <u>There are a variety of ways to measure promotion efforts.</u>

First, you may measure awareness by your target market. (9) <u>Anticipation of the event may be tantamount to ultimate participation</u>. Next, you may measure actual attendance and the resulting investment. (10) <u>Finally, you may measure the post event attitudes of the event promotional activity</u>. Did the promotions you designed persuade the participants or guests to attend the event?

B. Multiple Choices

• Dialogue 1

Tape script:

Woman: I want to know something abut the indoor advertising for the exhibition.

Man: The indoor advertisements fall into several categories：one is indoor booth billboard, which can vary; others are indoor TV screens and indoor advertising. Which kind are you interested in?

Woman: How 's the indoor booth billboard?

Man: If the style is very interesting, the effect can be quite Good. Old customers can find you quickly and new customers see you. For example, last year we adopted the lights, which had an excellent effect. You must choose a form of advertising in accordance with your budget.

Woman: Thank you for the explanation and suggestion. We will take them into consideration.Dialogue 2.

Tape script:

Man: Ms. Brown, I need a show box, what can I do?

Woman: A standard booth seldom has a show box. If you need one, you can rent it at the information desk of the exhibition hall. In addition, you can rent lights or other lamps and lanterns, flowers and plants.

(At the Information Desk, Miss Zhang is on duty.)

Woman: What can I do for you?

Man: Excuse me, can I rent a show box, lights and flowers here?

Woman: Yes. Please fill in this form, Including your booth number and the size and the amount of the things you want. After that, please settle accounts at Window 2. We will send what you need to your booth in an hour.

Man: Thank you!Dialogue 3.

Tape script:

Woman: Hello, Mr. Wang. This is Li Ming from Oriental Construction Company. We have met before. Do you still remember me?

Man: Yes, Miss Li. How are things going? You must be calling to ask about our construction exhibition. Would you like to join us this year?

Woman: That's right. What's the price for a booth this year?

Man: A standard booth costs RMB 4500 yuan. However, it is cheaper on the upper floor.

Woman: This is the third time we will take part in the exhibition. Can you give me a special price?

Man: I know. SInce you are old friends, I'm going to give you the maximum discount.

Woman: Thank you. I'll sign up now. And the down payment will be sent to your account in a few days. I will talk to you later in detail about the exact booth we are going to rent.

Man: Any time.Dialogue 4.

Tape script:

Man: Miss, you seem to be quite interested in our cotton textiles. What can I do for you?

Woman: I like cotton textiles from China very much. Could you show me some of your products, please?

Man: Fine. What kinds are you interested in? Textiles made from 100% cotton?

Woman: Yes, 100% cotton. I want to have a look at some samples.

Man: This way please. You see, we have pajamas, bed gowns, bathrobes, under linen, overcoats and cheongsams.

Woman: Oh, they are very beautiful. Is this cheongsam made from cotton, too?

Man: You are right.

Woman: What does this pattern mean?

Man:	It is a traditional Chinese pattern, which signifies luck and happiness.
Woman:	It is so pretty. I am interested in it. Of course, I am not ready to buy yet, but I will contact you as soon as possible. Thank you for the information.
Man:	You are welcome and please keep in touch.

Answers:

1.A 2.C 3.B 4.B 5.D 6.C 7.D 8.D 9.C 10.C 11.B 12.B

C. Passage Dictation

Tape script:

LinuxWorld Conference & Expo is the No. 1 marketplace for companies that sell, market or promote Linux-Based products, services, applications and solutions. Experiencing astounding growth, it's the largest gathering of open source professionals in the world. Linux adoption has been, and continues to be, nothing short of meteoric.

A November 2002 CIO survey found 54% of the respondents agree that Open Source will be their dominant platform in five years or less. Exhibiting at LinuxWorld enables you to present your entire line of products and services to attendees who run applications on both Open Source and proprietary platforms.

LinuxWorld Exhibitors enjoy numerous benefits:

-Speaking opportunity in the Linux Product Education Theatre

-Logo and link on show homepage

-Editorial in show preview

-Logo on all printed show material

-One time pre-show or post-show dedicated e-mail shot to pre-reg list

-100 word Inclusion plus hyperlink in show update e-mail

-One time access to pre-reg list for pre-show paper mailing

Section 2 Interpretation Activities

A. Sentence Interpretation

1. First, find out the equivalents of the following words.

virtually		導航線路	
target audience		電子文獻	
gauge		超文字媒體	
exhibitors manual		獲取	

2. Read the following to your partner for him or her to put them down in Chinese or English.

1. Information presented virtually could then also be used for educational purposes.

2. Obtain a list of exhibitors from the organizer, to determine whether the show covers your particular industry.

3. Obtain a list of show visitors from the organizer, to see if the visitors are your target audience.

4. Speak to companies who exhibited at the last show, to gauge how successful it was.

5. Read your exhibitors manual carefully. You will find all the information you need to make ordering things easy.

6. 虛擬展覽由數條導航線路構成。

7. 真實展覽與虛擬展覽兩種展覽方式各有千秋。

8. 資源中心圖書館收集了會議與活動管理所需的資訊。

9. 資源圖書館裡的有些資訊必須得到 ACCA 辦公室同意方可進入，但我們也提供越來越多的電子文獻，您可以立刻獲取。

10. 超文字媒體的可能性允許我們以一種嶄新的方式展示一種展品的文化背景。

B. Passage Interpretation

1. First, find out the equivalents of the following words.

information technology.	
明確的優勢	
真實性	
虛擬展覽	
適合	

2. Read the following passages to yourself and render them into Chinese or English.

• Passage 1

Information has value and ought to be organized and managed like other organizational resources. Information management can be defined as: the effective management of the information resources (internal and external) of an organization through the proper application of information technology. Convention and exhibition industry is at a certain extent a kind of information industry in which the importance of information management appear clearer.

Your Answer

_____

_____

_____

_____

_____

_____

_____

_____

_____

• Passage 2

虛擬和現實兩種展覽方式夠各有其明確的優勢。兩種展覽中的展品是相同的，但適合它們的具體展示的方法卻各不相同。現實展覽取決於展品的真實性，而虛擬展覽卻提供了一種把有關展品的不同資訊連結起來的可能。

Your Answer

_____

_____

_____

_____

_____

_____

_____

_____

Reference Answers

A. Sentence Interpretation

1.

virtually	以虛擬方式	導航線路	lines of navigation
target audience	目標觀眾	電子文獻	electronic document
gauge	評估	超文字媒體	hypermedia
exhibitors manual	參展商手冊	獲取	access

2.

1. 以虛擬方式展示的資訊還具有教育的用途。

2. 從組織者那裡獲取一張參展商名錄，以便確定展覽是否涵蓋您的商業領域。

3. 從展覽組織者那裡要一份展覽觀眾名錄，以便確定這些觀眾是否是您的目標觀眾。

4. 與上次參展的公司交流，評估展覽的成功程度。

5. 認真閱讀您的參展商手冊。您會發現裡面有您便捷訂購東西所需的所有資訊。

6. The virtual exhibition comprises several lines of navigation.

7. Each of the two kinds of exhibitions, virtual and real, has its specific strengths.

8. The Resource Center Library is a collection of information pertaining to conference and event management.

9. Some of the information from the Resource Library must be requested from the ACCA office, but we have a growing number of electronic documents that you can access immediately.

10. The possibilities of hypermedia allow a new way of presenting an exhibit in its cultural context.

B. Passage Interpretation

1.

information technology.	資訊技術

明確的優勢	specific strength
真實性	authenticity
虛擬展覽	virtual exhibition
適合	adopt to

2.

• Passage 1

資訊是具有價值德資源，它應該和其他組織資源一樣得到組織和管理。資訊管理可以被定義為：通過正確應用資訊技術使一個組織的資訊資源（內部和外部資源）得到有效管理。會議和展覽業在某種程度上可以說是一種資訊產業。資訊資源管理因而更顯重要。

• Passage 2

Each of the two kinds of exhibitions, virtual and real, has its specific strengths. Both exhibitions deal with the same objects, but present them in a way that is specifically adapted to the respective medium. While the real exhibition depends on the authenticity of the objects, the virtual one offers the possibility to interlink different pieces of information.

Section 3 Speaking Activities

A. Specialized Terms

Match the expressions on the left with the best Chinese equivalent on the right.

1. exhibition directory	A. 服務指南
2. exhibit prospectus	B. 半島形展位
3. gross square feet	C. 總面積
4. booth number	D. 攤位號碼
5. corner booth	E. 角落展位
6. island booth	F. 產品資訊表
7. peninsula booth	G. 護照申請表
8. service kit	H. 展位租金
9. space rate	I. 貴賓參觀卡
10.product and brand information	J. 參觀指南

| 11. passport request form | K. 參展資訊指南 |
| 12. VIP visitor invitation | L. 島形展位 |

B. Sample Conversation

Listen and read aloud.

Situation: The Auto Expo project manager of the Galaxy Exhibition Company is discussing the project comparative word done by the planning staff, Peter, Tom, Sam and Cherry.

Manager: Is everybody here? Yes, now begins our meeting. Today we shall focus on the project comparative work you've done earlier. Let's begin with Peter.

Peter: OK. Comparing all previous Auto Expos with our present project, the biggest difference is size. They had more exhibitors than those to be expected of ours. Take for example the Auto Sourcing Expo 2001, it had about 800 exhibitors.

Tom: And we won't be competitive in terms of venue. As it was, most of the Auto Expos were held in world-renowned exhibition centers, like Hanover.

Manager: What do you think of it, Sam?

Sam: I quite agree with them. In fact, there is one more point we cannot neglect. At the last Expo, the suppliers were all world leading automotive parts manufacturers.

Manager: You mean there will be fewer exhibitors to ours just because of our infamous venue?

Sam: Perhaps. Our revenue depends largely upon the number of exhibitors.

Cherry: But on the other hand, we can offer larger exhibition area. There'll be 6,000 square meters.

Manager: True. As one big advantage, the area is divided into 3 sections. Besides the sourcing and supplier exhibitor sections, we can also offer meeting rooms for the sourcing exhibitors.

Cherry: And adding to the competitiveness, sourcing exhibitors can be prearranged for one-on-one meetings with suppliers.

Manager: Right you are. Moreover, the reversed on-site purchasing allows the buyers to set up their own pavilions, while the suppliers are free to choose on site.

Cherry: Really. I'm just coming to that. The buyers exhibit products, images and blueprints by the most effective means, and the local suppliers can also display export-level products to meet multinational prospects with the lowest cost.

Sam: What smart ideas! We call it 'double-win'.

Manager: Yes. You can never overstate it.

Peter: So in this way, we will gain a lion's share by offering Good services.

Manager: You bet. Comparatively speaking, I believe our project is to achieve greater success than we expected. Work hard, ladies and gentlemen, our efforts will not be unfruitful.

C. Functional Expressions

Read aloud and practice with your partner.

Talking about similarities and differences

They had more exhibitors than those to be expected of ours.

Comparing all the previous Auto Expos, the biggest difference is size.

The Supertechnology Show is more expensive than Power Coating Europe.

There are four times as many exhibitors at CES as at Coating Europe.

Another difference is that these shows represent two separate markets for us.

The main similarity is that many of the big name companies will be exhibiting at both Expos.

What the buyer will achieve will equal to that at 30 traditional exhibitions.

Talking about advantages and disadvantages

And adding to the competitiveness, sourcing exhibitors can be prearranged for one-on-one meetings with suppliers.

One big advantage of exhibiting at ADIPEC is that we can meet retailers from all over the country.

As one big advantage, the area is divided into 3 sections.

But on the other hand, we can offer larger exhibition area.

And adding to the competitiveness, sourcing exhibitors can be prearranged for one-on-one meetings with suppliers.

The only drawback of ADIPEC is the cost. It's going to be quite expensive.

D. Speaking Up

Render the following into English by using as many language skills learnt as possible

1. 展覽的主辦者會向每位元參展者提供參展資訊手冊。

2. 參展手冊包含申請表和合約、說明展位元數目和位置的展區攤位圖，以及展覽公司可提供的所有服務。

3. 對於展廳的設計者來說，到會展中心繪製展廳的比例圖，其意義不僅僅是對展廳做一個測量。

4. 如果將展覽廳內那些大柱子或其他支撐結構的干擾作用考慮進來，實際展位元數目就會減少。

5. 根據專業展覽公司設計的圖樣，會議籌畫者能確定可以出租多少展位和幾種類型的展位。

E. Role-play

Practice the conversation in English according to the situation.

• Situation

A: You are applying for the position of engineer of a convention center in Shanghai. The prospective boss is asking you some questions about building a convention and exhibition information system. Try to give appropriate answers.

B: You are the manager of information department of a convention center in Shanghai. You are interviewing a recruit applying for the position of an engineer. Ask some questions about building a convention and exhibition information system.

Reference Answers

A. Specialized Terms

1. J 2. K 3. C 4. D. 5. E 6. L 7. B 8. A 9. H 10. F 11. G 10. I

D. Speaking Up

1. The expo organizer should provide exhibition manual for each exhibitor.

2. Exhibition Manual contains registration form and contract, specifies the number of booths and the booth layout in the exhibit area, and offer services available to exhibitors.

3. For exhibit hall designers, drawing a scaled layout of the exhibition hall is more than measuring the hall.

4. Based on the layout provided by professinoal exhibition companies, meeting planners can determine how many and what type of stands to let.

Chapter 5
Visiting Foreign Exhibitors 拜會贊助商

▌ Section 1 Listening Activities

Go over the following words and expressions before listening to the tape.

starter home	房車
promotional literature	促銷宣傳資料
contributed papers	提交論文
green house effect	溫室效應
shuttle bus	定點定時班車
boom	繁榮
spotlight	聚光燈
exhilarating	令人興奮的
diversity	多樣化
COMDEX（Computer Dealer's Expo)	電腦經銷商博覽會
EXPO COMM (Exposition of Communications)	國際通信展

A. Spot Dictation

There are many (1) _____ to be (2) _____ from exhibiting at a show. Typically held on an annual or (3) _____ basis, it is an exciting, (4) _____ event: everyone is wondering what it will be like, who shall be there, what will be different and new, what may happen and so on. Just by being there, you can help to establish, change or maintain (5) _____s in the field. In many instances you almost have to (6) _____ to 'keep up with the Joneses'. Your (7) _____ _____.

Depending on the size of your stand, (8) _____ _____.___.. Larger items – everything from an office photocopier to mocked-up, one-bedroom starter home – may be shown too. Your products can be displayed as you want them to be seen, under controlled conditions.

They (9) _____ Supporting material from pattern swatches to promotional literature is readily available to hand. (10) _____

_____.

B. Multiple Choices

Directions: *In this section you will hear several Dialogues. After each Dialogue, there are some questions. Listen to the Dialogues carefully and choose the most appropriate answer to each question from the four choices marked A, B, C and D.*

● **Dialogue 1**

1. Where is this conversation most probably taking place?

   A. At a conference center.

   B. At an airport.

   C. At a restaurant.

   D. At a hotel.

2. What is the theme of the event?

   A. A conference on green house effect.

   B. A meeting on soil protection.

   C. A meeting on water protection. D. A seminar on air pollution.

3. What is Peter's present research scope? A. The tourism research.

   B. The environment research.

   C. The chemistry research.

   D. The electronics research.

4. What is Susan asked to do at the conference on green house effect to be held in China?

   A. To read her paper on the green house effect.

   B. To tell a story.

   C. To make a introductory speech.

   D. To preside at the meeting.

●Dialogue 2

5. What event will they be attending in Hong Kong in November?

　A. The Travel Expo.

　B. A book show.

　C. An international travel products show.

　D. The Paris travel products show.

6. What is the biggest difference between the New York travel products show and the Paris travel products show?

　A. There are a smaller number of attendees in New York show. B. There are a larger number of attendees in New York show.

　C. Big name travel firms will be at the New York show. D. Big name travel firms will be at the Paris show.

7. Which show have they decided to put on?

　A. A show in New York.

　B. A show in Paris.

　C. A show in England.

　D. Not mentioned.

8. When will the show be held next year? A. In May.

　B. In November.

　C. In September.

　D. In March.

●Dialogue 3

9. Why is there a boom in the exhibition industry in China?

　A. More and more exhibition centers are being established.

　B. More and more exhibition companies are being set up.

　C. Revenue from exhibition industry has been rising steadily.

　D. All of the above

10. Which of the following sectors will benefit greatly by the World Expo 2010?

　A. Hotels.

　B. Agriculture.

　C. Tourism.

D. Finance.

11. Why isn't the World Expo merely thought of as a trade fair or an industrial exhibition?

    A. Culture is manifest in what people say and do.

    B. Exhibits themselves represent different cultures.

    C. Exhibitions display something of beauty or value.

    D. All of the above.

C. Passage Dictation

Directions: *In this section, you will hear a passage. Listen carefully and write down what you hear on the tape.*

_____

_____

_____

_____

_____

_____

_____

_____

_____

_____

_____

Tape script & Answers

A. Spot Dictation

Tape script:

There are many (1) <u>benefits</u> to be (2) <u>derived</u> from exhibiting at a show. Typically held on an annual or (3) <u>biannual</u> basis, it is an exciting, (4) <u>look-forward-to</u> event: everyone is wondering what it will be like, who shall be there, what will be different and new, what may happen and so on. Just by being there, you can help to establish, change or maintain (5) <u>your reputation and status</u> in the field. In many instances you almost have to (6) <u>be present</u> to 'keep up with the Joneses'. Your (7) <u>absence could be viewed – correctly or Incorrectly – as a bad sign, possibly even of impending business failure.</u>

Depending on the size of your stand, (8) <u>you may display a fuller range of Goods than your sales team can take out on the road.</u> Larger items – everything from an office photocopier to mocked-up, one-bedroom starter home (房車) – may be shown too. Your products can be displayed as you want them to be seen, under controlled conditions. They (9) <u>may also be demonstrated, touched, tested, examined and operated by visitors.</u> Supporting material from pattern swatches to promotional literature is readily available to hand. (10) <u>In theory, you can create the perfect sales environment.</u>

B. Multiple Choices

Tape script:

● **Dialogue 1**

Woman:	Hi, Peter. How nice to see you here.
Man:	Hello Susan. It's a small world. It's years sInce we last met. How are things with you?
Woman:	Nothing special, except that I'm busy with meetings recently.
Man:	And it's also the reason for what has brought you here today, isn't it?
Woman:	Yeah, yeah. To be exact, I'm attending a seminar on air pollution. I contributed one paper on this issue and I'm going to read my paper during the seminar. And you are attending the meeting here?
Man:	Yes. I happened to find myself interested in environment research one year ago. My paper on this issue was selected by the seminar.
Woman:	I'm so glad to hear that. I bet you didn't have much trouble with your switch, because, I know, you are so talented a guy.
Man:	You are flattering me. Oh, tell me your plan for the coming three months.

Woman:	There will be a conference on green house effect to be held in China, and I will be making a keynote speech on that topic.
Man:	I will be flying there, too.
Woman:	I'm looking forward to meeting you again in China.
Man:	Here comes the shuttle bus for Hilton Hotel. Are you staying in the Hilton?
Woman:	Exactly. There we go.
Man:	Yes, let's.

● **Dialogue 2**

Man:	As you know, we'll be exhibiting at the Travel Expo in Hong Kong in November, but we need to make plans for one other international travel products show next year.
Woman:	Well, what is our budget?
Man:	Unfortunately, this is a tight year for us, so we can do Hong Kong show and only one other big show. You have studied the documents about the travel products show in New York and the one in Paris. So, what do you think?
Woman:	Comparing both shows, the biggest difference is size. There are four times as Many attendees at the New York Show.
Man:	Yes, and another difference is that these shows clearly represent two separate markets for us.
Woman:	The main similarity I see between the two shows is that Many of the big name travel firms will be at both shows.
Man:	I think the U.S. customers are our major target outside Asia at this point.
Woman:	All right then, why don't we get a booth and put on a Good show in New York?
Man:	Sounds like a Good idea.
Woman:	Are you available in May?
Man:	Yes, I am certainly available in May. I'd like to work on the design of our booth in New York.

● **Dialogue 3**

Man:	I've sensed a boom in the exhibition industry in China.

Woman:	You are really keeping your eyes open. Yet more and more exhibition centers are being established.
Man:	And more exhibition companies, too.
Woman:	Right. In shanghai, for example, there has been a steady rise of revenue from exhibition industry.
Man:	Especially sInce Shanghai won the sponsorship of hosting the 2010 World Expo. I'm still excited when I recall that exhilarating moment.
Woman:	So am I. Imagine Shanghai will become the place where spotlights shine, and a world of people will flow into this city.
Man:	The World Expo will greatly benefit China's industry and trade, I believe.
Woman:	You bet it will. What is more, China's tourism will profit by the World Expo, too. SInce foreign visitors and exhibitors will have to be housed, fed and transported, hotels and restaurants are among the beneficial sectors.
Man:	Now I understand why the World Expo cannot be merely thought of as a trade fair or an industrial exhibition. What people do and say pertains to a type of culture. So the Expo will become a place where a diversity of cultures are exchanged.
Woman:	You said it. Cultures are also represented by exhibits themselves. Although exhibits are brought together temporarily for the expo, they display or demonstrate something of beauty or value.

Answers

1. B; 2. D; 3. B; 4. C; 5. A; 6. B; 7. A; 8. A; 9. D; 10. C; 11. D;

C. Passage Dictation

Tape script:

COMDEX UK will be a technology trade show of unprecedented scope and quality. This event will bring together COMDEX, Networld and EXPO COMM, creating the first−ever forum focused on converging information technology, networking and telecommunications markets.

COMDEX is the IT industry's NO. 1 showcase and launching pad for new and emerging technologies. It is the only business-to-business computer exposition in the UK. Networld is the industry's leading showcase and conference dedicated to internetworking technologies, applications and solutions. EXPO COMM is the premier worldwide event for telecommunications infrastructure technologies, communications services, and related applications.

This joint exhibition and conference allows industry professionals to see all of the latest technologies in their fields and network with IT directors, developers, technical specialists, IT consultants, and industry analysts.

Section 2 Interpretation Activities

A. Sentence Interpretation

1. First, find out the equivalents of the following words.

1 direct marketing		6 資料庫	
2 special interest media		7 回饋率	
3 news release		8 印刷媒體	
4 layout		9 促銷	
5 mega event		10 受眾	

2. Read the following to your partner for him or her to put them down in Chinese or English.

1. Promoting through the media can reach the widest audience quickly, but it may not be focused on or targeted at a certain group of people.

2. Both approaches will take time and money, but it is possible to get support from media in the form of stories about your event for free or low cost if your event is a large or major or important gathering for some industry.

3. News media may carry a story about your event if the event is special in some way. Send a press release to the media telling them why your event is the first or biggest of its kind, or the most important in your industry.

4. You advertisement needs to be edited, the language checked and double-checked for errors, and the design checked for layout clarity and key information.

5. Response rates will depend on the interest level of the target, the beauty and suitability of the direct marketing piece, and the timing of the delivery to the target person or group.

6. 直接推廣方式則非常集中和具針對性，可以使目標人群看到你傳遞的資訊，但是這種方式成本較高，而且需要時間去處理。

7. 如果你已經有或能夠建立自己的聯絡資料資料庫，這可能是推廣活動的最佳方式，而且得到的回應率也是最高的。

8. 如今的媒體包括印刷品、電台、電視台和互聯網。兩種主要媒體分別是新聞和專業行業媒體。

9. 專業行業媒體有多種形式，例如行業雜誌，宣傳所屬行業的電視或電台節目，或專注於所屬行業或利益集團的網站等。

10. 如今通過電子郵件形式直接推廣最為普遍，但必須確保目標讀者同意接收經篩選的此類資訊。

B. Passage Interpretation

1. First, find out the equivalents of the following words.

potential revenue stream	
inventory	
統計特徵	
投資回報	

2. Read the following passages to yourself and render them into Chinese or English.

● Passage 1

　　From an event's perspective, sponsorship often (but not always) represents a significant potential revenue stream. Yet, sponsorship are fast becoming business partnerships that offer resources beyond money. To succeed in the sponsorship stakes, event organizers must thoughtfully develop policies and strategies, providing a clear framework for both events and sponsors to decide on the value and suitability of potential partnerships. Having an inventory of the event assets available for sale is an important starting point for those seeking sponsorship.

Your Answer

_____

_____

_____

_____

_____

_____

_____

_____

• **Passage 2**

　　在說服一家企業贊助活動時，瞭解其市場和目標是至關重要的。企業客戶的統計特徵應該與活動參與者的統計特徵相一致。做好準備，向企業準確地說明其（贊助的）投資回報。如果你能表現出理解企業的需求，企業方面會更加願意傾聽活動是如何滿足這些需求的。

Your Answer

_____

_____

_____

_____

_____

_____

_____

_____

Reference Answers

A. Sentence Interpretation

1.

| 1 direct marketing | 直接行銷 | 6 資料庫 | database |
| 2 special interest media | 專業行業媒體 | 7 回饋率 | response rate |

3 news release	新聞發佈稿	8 印刷媒體	print media
4 layout	版面設計 \ 佈局圖	9 促銷	promotion
5 mega event	特大活動	10 受眾	audience

2.

1. 通過媒體推廣可以迅速接觸到最廣泛的受眾，但是可能會不集中或沒有針對一個特定的人群。

2. 兩種方式都需要花費時間和金錢。但是，如果是規模龐大的活動或是某個行業的重要盛會，那麼你也許會得到媒體的支持，媒體會免費或低價為活動作宣傳。

3. 如果活動在某方面有特別之處，新聞媒體可能會對其進行報導。向媒體發佈新聞稿，告訴他們本次活動在同類活動中堪稱首次或規模最大的理由。

4. 廣告需要編輯，語言需要校對、校對、再校對以避免錯誤，佈局圖和重要資訊需要設計核對。

5. 回應率的高低取決於直接推廣文案的針對程度、美觀性和適用性，以及向目標人群發送時機的把握。應用這種動態發展的技術，以使你的活動在整個二十一世紀始終保持競爭力。

6. Direct marketing can be very focused on and targeted at the group you want to see your message, but it can be quite expensive and take time to set up well.

7. If you have or can build your own database of contacts interested in your event, this will probably be the best way to promote your event and will result in the highest response rate.

8. Media Includes print, radio, television, and the Internet now. Two main kinds of media are news, and special interest medi 阿 .

9. Special interest media come in all kinds. Magazines about your industry, TV or radio programs relating to your industry, or Web sites devoted to your industry or interest group are all examples.

10. Direct marketing by email is now the most popular, but make sure your target agrees to receive the messages through an opt-in list.

B. Passage Interpretation

1.

potential revenue stream	潛在收入來源
inventory	詳細目錄

統計特徵	demographics
投資回報	return on investment

2.

● **Passage 1**

從活動的角度來看，贊助往往（但不總是）代表著巨大的潛在收入來源。不過，贊助越來越成為一種商業合作行為，即贊助的是資源而不僅僅是錢。為成功地獲得贊助，活動組織者必須制訂完善的方針和戰略，為活動和贊助商確立清晰的合作框架，以明確合作的價值和可行性。有成形的活動可供銷售，是尋求贊助的重要起點。

● **Passage 2**

When convIncing a company to sponsor your event, it's critical that you know their market and their goals. The demographics of their potential customers should match the demographics of your attendees. Be prepared to explain exactly what they can expect in return for their investment. If you can show them that you can understand their needs, they'll be more willing to listen to how your event support those needs.

Section 3 Speaking Activities

A. Specialized Terms

Match the expressions on the left with the best Chinese equivalent on the right.

1.	open days(time, period)	A.	安保
2.	rental charge	B.	標準裝配
3.	subject	C.	地面負荷
4.	hospitality	D.	獨立展覽
5.	booth area	E.	公用設施服務
6.	floor plan	F.	公展期
7.	floor loading(covering)	G.	過道寬度
8.	aisle width	H.	接待 / 招待
9.	main dimension	I.	平面圖

10. standard fitting	J. 展位面積
11. security	K. 整體規格
12. free-standing exhibits	L. 主題 / 被調查者
13. access	M. 准入
14. utility service	N. 租金

B. Sample Conversation

Listen and read aloud.

Situation: Mr. Li and Mrs. Ding are talking about the sponsorship package for the 2nd International Toy Exhibition.

Woman: Good morning. What a pleasure to see you again, Mr. Li.

Man: Good morning, Mrs. Ding. Nice to meet you too. It's said you are organizing the 2nd International Toy Exhibition .

Woman: Yes, and that's why I come here. To be frank, we are seeking some sponsors now. Are you interested in it?

Man: Well, we sponsored the 1st International Toy Exhibition last year, and really got a lot. Many consumers recognized our products and brand although we were a newly founded toy company at that time.

Woman: Yes, we cooperated with each other very well. So you are our fist choice for sponsors this time .

Man: Good. Would you please tell me some details about this year's exhibition? What are your objectives?

Woman: Here is the sponsorship package. In general, we hope to have 600 domestic and 400 international exhibitors this time, and attract about 10,000 visitors.

Man: Sounds wonderful. I will read this package in detail later. By the way, are there any other sponsors involved?

Woman: Actually, we try to cooperate with different kinds of sponsors according to their interest and levels of contribution.

Man: How much money is requested for title sponsor?

Woman: RMB 100,000 yuan.

Man: That's really reasonable. Thank you very much for the information. I have to talk this with my teammates and let you know our decision in two weeks.

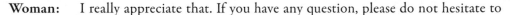

Woman: I really appreciate that. If you have any question, please do not hesitate to contact me.

Man: We will. Thanks again. Goodbye.

Woman: Goodbye. Thanks for your time.

C. Functional Expressions

Read aloud and practice with your partner.

How to elicit questions politely	Response
Can I help you?	Yes, I'd like to know some general information about your event
May I help you?	Yes, we'd like to know your sponsorship selection criteria.
Is there anything else I can do for you?	How to complete the sponsorship application form?

Frequently asked questions by potential sponsors

How much money is requested?

How will it be spent?

How many people will be present at the event?

What are the target audience for your event (for example, age, gender, employment statue, etc)?

How will the event be promoted?

Has the event been conducted in the past?

Do you intend repeating this event?

D. Speaking Up

Render the following into English by using as many language skills learnt as possible.

1. 贊助商冠名需多少錢？
2. 有多少人參加這次活動？
3. 請問還有什麼我可以幫忙的嗎？
4. 請問活動的目標。
5. 市場是怎樣的？

E. Role-play

Practice the conversations according to the situations.

• **Situation 1**

Mr. Smith is from a company who would like to take pat in the sponsorship of a show. Mrs. Li is the show manager. They are talking about what items the company chooses to sponsor and in return, what benefits the company is likely to obtain. Please try the Dialogue with your partner.

• **Situation 2**

Two companies sponsored a volunteer effort to clean up the city's park. Two persons from the companies are discussing this event.

• **Situation 3**

Two employees from two companies who have sponsored a meeting on information technology, are discussing what their companies contributed to the meeting and how they feel about the decisions of their respective company. Please try the Dialogue using your real names in pairs.

• **Situation 4**

Rose is working at the Sunshine Convention Service. Now she is answering a phone call from Henry Smith who wants to get some information about sponsoring a meeting.

Refenecne Answer

A. Specialized Terms

1.F 2.N 3.L 4.H 5.J 6.I 7.C 8.G 9 K 10.B 11 A 12 D 13. M 14. E

D. Speaking Up

1. How much money is requested for title sponsors?
2. How many people will participating in this event?

3. Is there anything else I can do for you?
4. What are the goal of your event?
5. What are the target audience for your event?

Chapter 6
Negotiating on Exhibiting Space 展位談判

▌ Section 1 Listening Activities

Go over the following words and expressions before listening to the tape.

reliable		a.	可靠的
cater		v.	備辦餐飲
skeptic		a.	懷疑的
constraint		n.	制約因素
liability		n.	責任
impose		v.	強加於
household utensil			家用器皿
forwarder		n.	運輸公司
warehouse		n.	倉庫
get acquainted with			熟悉
press conference			新聞發佈會
Hannover			漢諾威（城市名）

A. Spot Dictation

Event resources generally Include people, time, finances , (1)_____, and physical assts. Although each is important, each is also extremely (2)_____ . Occasionally, someone will tell me that they have (3)_____

resources for their event. I am (4)_____ this because of the economic theory which states that you must learn to allocate scarce resources to (5)_____. No matter how many resources you have, the fact is that they are always limited. The way you (6)_____ is through careful and creative allocation.

The event manager must be able to (7)_____ for their event. Furthermore, the event manager has to attest that these resources are reliable. (8)_____ .Therefore, after every effort is made to verify the quality of an event resource such as entertainment or catering or venue, (9)_____

_____: "The information contained herein

is deemed to be reliable but not guaranteed." (10)_____
_____ . Therefore, the event manager should do
what is reasonable and inform the client of the status of the level of reliability of the
information that he or she is providing.

B. Multiple Choices

Directions: *In this section you will hear several Dialogues. After each Dialogue, there
are some questions. Listen to the Dialogues carefully and choose the most
appropriate answer to each question from the four choices marked A, B, C
and D.*

● **Dialogue 1**

1. Where will this exhibition be held?
   A. Paris.
   B. London.
   C. Soul.
   D. Washington.

2. How many buying groups will come to this exhibition?
   A. 3000.
   B. 2000.
   C. 200.
   D. 3500.

3. What is the closing date of this exhibition?
   A. October 5th.
   B. October 15th.
   C. October 25th.
   D. October 20th.

● **Dialogue 2**

4. Why do people often choose booths on the ground floor?
   A. They are cheaper.
   B. They can catch more attentions.

C. They are easy to reach.

D. They can be easily taken care of.

5. Why can the exhibitor get that Good booth?

　　A. Because he would pay more for it.

　　B. Because there are many booths left.

　　C. Because he is one of the old customers to this exhibition.

　　D. Because someone cancelled their reservation.

6. Has the consultant made his decision to take the booth at last?

　　A. No.

　　B. Not mentioned.

　　C. Yes.

　　D. Not yet.

● **Dialogue 3**

7. Where should the forwarder company transport the display items from?

　　A. The warehouse.

　　B. The exhibitor's company.

　　C. The exhibition center.

　　D. The dock.

8. What should the exhibitor do before transportation?

　　A. Fill in some forms.

　　B. Make the reservation.

　　C. Pay transportation fee.

　　D. Have the items well prepared.

9. Which one of the following is not true according to the Dialogue?

　　A. The exhibition will be held in the World Trade Center .

　　B. He exhibitor is the old customer of this forwarder company.

　　C. The exhibitor can transport their displays one day before the exhibition.

　　D. After the exhibition, the displays should be transported back to our exhibitor's company.

• Dialogue 4.

10. What are the exhibits of Mr. Li's company according to the Dialogue?

    A. Kitchen utensils.

    B. Glass wares.

    C. Home appliances.

    D. Textiles.

11. What is purpose of the press conference?

    A. Promoting the sales.

    B. Building Good relationships with customers.

    C. Expanding the marketing.

    D. Strengthening the brand.

12. How many customers is Mr. Li acquainted with?

    A. 2.

    B. More than 200.

    C. 200.

    D. Less than 200.

C. Passage Dictation

Directions: *In this section, you will hear a passage. Listen carefully and write down what you hear on the tape.*

_____

_____

_____

_____

_____

_____

_____

_____

Tape script & Answers:

A. Spot Dictation

Tape script:

Event resources generally Include people, time, finances, (1) <u>technology,</u> and physical assts. Although each is important, each is also extremely (2) <u>scarce</u>. Occasionally, someone will tell me that they have (3) <u>unlimited</u> resources for their event. I am (4) <u>skeptic about</u> this because of the economic theory which states that you must learn to allocate scarce resources to (5) <u>achieve maximum benefit</u>. No matter how many resources you have, the fact is that they are always limited. The way you (6) <u>stretch your resources</u> is through careful and creative allocation.

The event manager must be able to (7) <u>identify the most appropriate resources</u> for their event. Furthermore, the event manager has to attest that these resources are reliable. (8) <u>This is not always possible, due to time constraints</u> .Therefore, after every effort is made to verify the quality of an event resource such as entertainment or catering or venue,(9) <u>the event manager may wish to Include the following statement in the proposal to reduce his or her liability</u>: "The information contained herein is deemed to be reliable but not guaranteed." (10) <u>It is impossible to verify and confirm every resource within the brief time constraints imposed by most events</u>. Therefore, the event manager should do what is reasonable and inform the client of the status of the level of reliability of the information that he or she is providing.

B. Multiple Choices

Tape script:

● **Dialogue 1**

Woman: Could you talk about the International Textile Material Exhibition this time?

Man: The exhibition will be held from October 15th to October 20th in Paris.

Woman: Oh, I see. How Many booths will you provide?

Man: An estimated of 2000. The buyers are 3500 professional buying groups from more than 200 countries and regions.

Woman:	That sounds Good.
Man:	There has been great number of contracts and orders in previous exhibitions.
Woman:	Thank you.
Man:	My pleasure.

• Dialogue 2

Man:	Ms. Brown, after serious consideration, our company has decided to take part in the International Household Utensil Exhibition and has made me in charge of the work here.
Woman:	I am glad that your company decided to take part in the exhibition. You won't be disappointed.
Man:	Thank you, Ms. Brown. But I don't know what kind of booth is best.
Woman:	People often choose booths on the ground floor, which are distInct and attract more customers.
Man:	Could you recommend some to me?
Woman:	You are lucky that a company which had booked a booth cancelled its participation in the exhibition. The booth is in the middle of the second line facing the gate-A215. I think it suits you.
Man:	Fine. I will take the booth and I'll fax the registration form tomorrow.
Woman:	Thank you.

• Dialogue 3

Woman:	When can I transport the display items to the World Trade Center?
Man:	Two days before the exhibition. Do you need us to deliver your display items this year?
Woman:	That's fine. This year, we need the forwarder company to transport the display items directly from our warehouse to the exhibition, and after the exhibition, transport them back to our company.
Man:	So the transportation will involve road and rail. You must arrange the transportation in advance.
Woman:	We will take care and prepare the items beforehand.
Man:	We will come to deliver your items on time.
Woman:	Thank you.
Man:	My pleasure.

● **Dialogue 4.**

Woman:　Mr. Li, what are the results of the exhibition?

Man:　Not bad.

Woman:　Could you give me some details?

Man:　We have established business relationships with two new clients, who ordered RMB 20 million yuan of silk skirts.

Woman:　That sounds Good.

Man:　I also got acquainted with more than 200 customers.

Woman:　Oh, wow.

Man:　Customers made more than ten suggestions. There, I held a product showing meeting and a press conference. As a result, our brand has been strengthened.

Woman:　Very Good!

Man:　Here is the results analysis. I hope the visitors at the exhibition can be our real buyers in 3 to 6 months. What's more, we learned a lot from other exhibitors.

Woman:　You are right. I think you've done an excellent job.

Answers:

1.A　2.D　3.D　4.B　5.D　6.C　7.A　8.D　9.C　10.D　11.D　12.B

C. Passage Dictation

Tape script:

Exhibition executives can be subdivided into senior management and operation staff. International standards have been established for exhibition systems, but we need to localize these international rules and tailor them to China. So, we sent representatives to the Hannover EXPO in Germany, who came back with observations of how important cooperation was in the Hannover EXPO. Everyone took care of his/her job well and everything went smoothly. If, during the planning period from now to 2005, we work efficiently, create a detailed plan and maintain normal operations, everyone should be able to contribute effectively. Right now, there are many outstanding Chinese individuals, but most of them lack the ability to work in a team. Therefore, the focus of training should be on improving teamwork and coordination.

Section 2 Interpretation Activities

A. Sentence Interpretation

1. First, find out the equivalents of the following words.

1 newsletter		6 高消費階層的	
2 target market		7 名人	
3 public relations		8 廣告宣傳品	
4 collateral material		9 新聞發佈	
5 premium		10 戶外廣告	

2. Read the following to your partner for him or her to put them down in Chinese or English.

1. 才過一個月你的租場費就高出百分之二十五。
2. 這並不意外。你也知道現在是展覽旺季。展覽公司都爭著租用我們的展覽館。
3. 但是你們的價格和我從其他地方得到的價格相比還是高出許多。
4. 可是我們場地交通便利,而且還有全市面積最大的底樓展廳。
5. 是的,這我承認。然而,我覺得很難在這麼高的價格上說服參展商購買攤位。
6. 那麼,你認為什麼樣的價格是可以接受的呢?
7. 我覺得應該再降價 15%。
8. 考慮到我們以往的良好合作,我們給你 10% 的優惠吧。
9. 好吧,我們就成交了。

B. Passage Interpretation

1. First, find out the equivalents of the following words.

fam. trip		指定服務商	
proceed		裝潢公司	
installation		招攬生意	
move-in		總比沒有好	

2. Read the following passages and translate them into Chinese or English.

● Passage 1:

L: Good morning, Mr. Smith. I hope you enjoyed your fam. trip yesterday.

S: Good morning, Mr. Li. I did enjoy it. It was a wonderful trip.

L: I'm very glad to hear that. I suspect, however, we'd like to get down to business. How would you like to proceed with the negotiations?

S: Today, I would like to talk about the move-in with you. We have a plan to attend this exhibition organized by your company, but we still want to confirm some terms about move-in.

L: What terms do you want to confirm?

S: When are we supposed to finish the installation?

L: All exhibits must be constructed and decorated by 5 p.m. on the day before exhibit opening.

S: That's what we worry about. Because we might need to spend some time decorating the stand. The time limit is tense. Shall we move in earlier or finish it later?

L: That doesn't conform to our usual practice. Anyway, could you tell me how much earlier you want to move in?

S: 2 hours.

● **Passage 2:**

L: 兩個小時太多了。 我們無法接受。

S: 那多長時間是可以的呢？

L: 我們只能給半個小時。

S: 半個小時？太少了。

L: 我知道，可是這已經是我們公司規定內的可以做出最大讓步了。

S: 好吧。總比沒有好。我們會儘量在規定的時間內完成的。 第二個我們想確定的是關於裝潢公司的事情。根據展覽會的相關條款，你們公司指定了 FREEMAN 裝潢公司，那麼，我們可以帶我們自己的裝潢工人入場麼？

L: 可以。但是你們的工人任何時間都不能在場館內招攬生意。你們要對他們的行為負責。

S: 我明白你們的意思。

Reference Answers

A. Sentence Interpretation

1.

1 newsletter	時事通訊	6 高消費階層的	upscale

2 target market	目標市場	7 名人	celebrity
3 public relations	公共關係	8 廣告宣傳品	advertising specialty
4 collateral material	輔助宣傳材料	9 新聞發佈	news release
5 premium	贈品	10 戶外廣告	outdoor advertising

2.

1. Your venue rental rate is 25% higher than that one month ago.

2. There is no surprise. You know, it is the peak season of exhibitions. Exhibition companies are now all applying for spaces in our venue.

3. But your prices are still much higher than what we are offered by other venues.

4. As you can see, we are easily accessible and have this city's largest dispay area on the ground floor.

5. I know that's true. However, it will be hard for us to talk exhibitors into renting spaces of such a high price.

6. Could you tell me your idea of a reasonable price?

7. I think there should be another 15% discount.

8. For a Good start of our potential cooperation in the future, we can give you another 10% discount.

9. OK. That's the deal.

B. Passage Interpretation

1.

fam. trip	現場考察	指定服務商	official service contractor
proceed	繼續	裝潢公司	Decorating company
installation	搭建	招攬生意	solicit business
move-in	進展	總比沒有好	Better than nothing

2.

● **Passage 1:**

L： 史密斯先生，早上好。希望您喜歡昨天的實地考察旅行。

S： 李先生，早上好。我非常喜歡。這是一次很美好的旅行。

L： 我很高興你能喜歡。我想我們應該坐下來談生意了。你認為我們今天談甚麼呢？

S: 今天我想跟你們談談關於布展的事情。我們計畫參加此次你們公司主辦的展覽，可是我們還要確認一些關於布展的條款。

L: 你們想確認的是甚麼條款？

S: 我們甚麼時候就要完成布展？

L: 所有的展台必須在展覽正式開始的前一天下午五點之前佈置完畢。

S: 這正是我們擔心的。因為我們可能需要點時間來裝飾我們的展台。你們的時間限制太緊張了。我們是否可以提前進場或者延遲退場的時間呢？

L: 這不符合我們慣有的做法。不過，你們可以先告訴我你們想提前多長時間入場？

S: 兩個小時。

● **Passage 2:**

L: Two hours is too much! I don't think it is acceptable.

S: How much is possible?

L: What we can do is to offer half an hour.

S: Half an hour? That's little.

L: I know, but that is what we can do according to this exhibition rules.

S: Ok. Better than nothing. The second term we want to confirm is about the decorating company. According to the rules, your company has selected Freeman Decorating Company as the official service contractor. Can we take our decorating workers in?

L: Yes, you can. But your workers may not solicit business in the exhibit hall at any time. You must be responsible for the actions of them.

S: I see what you mean.

Section 3 Speaking Activities

A. Specialized Terms

Match the expressions on the left with the best Chinese equivalent on the right.

1. offer	A. 還價
2. counter offer	B. 實盤
3. rock-bottom/floor price	C. 報價
4. firm offer	D. 底價
5. transaction	E. 展出淨面積
6. call off (the deal)	F. 優惠條件

7. inquiry	G. 詢價
8. best terms	H. 特殊裝修光地展位
9. quotations	I. 做出讓步
10. make concessions	J. 不做（這筆）生意
11. exhibition net area	K. 生意
12. raw space with special decoration	L. 報盤

B. Sample Conversation

Listen and read aloud.

Situation: Li-Ming of the local exhibition center receives the Auto Expo project manager of the Galaxy Exhibition Company. The manager intends to discuss the price terms for reserving exhibition area with Mr. Li-Ming.

Li-Ming: Hello, Mr. Thompson. It's a pleasure to see you again so soon.

Manager: It's my pleasure to see you again, too. Mr. Li.

Li-Ming: Take a seat, please.

Manager: Thank you.

Li-Ming: Do you care for tea or coffee?

Manager: Tea, please. Thanks. Shall we get down to business right now?

Li-Ming: OK. I believe you have received our center's size catalogue and price list.

Manager: Yes, we have given it serious considerations and today I've come for the details about price terms. We found your price on the high side.

Li-Ming: I'm surprised to hear that. I think our prices are competitive. Hardly can you get such favorable prices from other exhibition centers.

Manager: Perhaps you are right. But it's really hard for us to rent it to our exhibitors at such a high price.

Li-Ming: What's your proposal then?

Manager: I suggest that there be 15% discount.

Li-Ming: What's the total area you have in your mind?

Manager: About 5,500 square meters.

Li-Ming: Which halls are you interested in?

Manager: They must be the Center Hall and its side rooms on the 1st floor, the entire second floor of No. 1 Eastern Hall.

Li-Ming: 5,500 square meters is certainly not a large area. But sInce it is the first business between you and us, you may have our 5% reduction.

Manager: It's impossible for me to accept that. Can we meet it halfway: a reduction of 10%?

Li-Ming: Your counter offer is not acceptable. We have never offered that before.

Manager: Well, if you insist, can you prolong the hall closing hours from 6:00p.m. to 7:30p.m. during the event free of charge?

Li-Ming: Yes, we can keep the hall open half an hour longer. For a Good start to our business relationship, we'll give you 5% discount and the free use of the halls from 6:00p.m. to 7:30p.m. during the event.

Manager: OK. Let's call it a deal.

C. Functional Expressions

Read aloud and practice with your partner.

- **Saying the prices offered are too high**

    We find your prices are on the high side.

    Your price is much higher than we were expecting to pay.

    Your price is not so attractive as that offered by other suppliers.

    Your price is out of line with the current market price.

    I'm so surprised to see that your price is almost 20% higher than last year's.

Asking for a counter offer

    Would you let us know your counter offer?

    What reasonable price do you have in your mind?

    What is your proposal?

    What do you think is a completive price?

    Could you tell me your idea of a reasonable price?

- **Bargaining for a lower price**

    Can we meet it halfway: a reduction of 10%?

    If you consider reducing the rental rates, I'll reserve a greater amount of exhibition space.

    If you insist on not making a discount, I can find lower prices elsewhere.

- **Agreeing to reduce the price**

  SInce it is the first business between you and us, you may have our 5% reduction.

  For a Good start to our business relationship, we'll give you 5% discount and the free use of the halls from 6:00p.m. to 7:30p.m. during the event.

  In view of our cooperation in the past, we accept your counter-offer.

  To encourage future business, we'll make an exception and give you a 8% discount.

  If you reserve enough large exhibition space, we're preparing to reduce the price by 8%.

- **Refusing to reduce the price**

  Your counter offer is not acceptable. We have never offered that before.

  We have offered you our rock-bottom price. We can't make any further concessions.

  I'm afraid there is no room to negotiate the price.

  This is really our floor price. If you can't accept it, I'm afraid we have to call the deal off.

D. Speaking Up

Understand the speaker's intention, and then fill in the blanks.

1. ——I believe you've studied out catalogue and price. Are you interested in some of our exhibition halls?

   ——_____.

   （用意：表示對方價格太高）

2. ——_____?

   （用意：請對方還價）

   ——I think you should at least reduce the rental by 15%

3. ——The best I can do is to give you a 10% discount.

   ——_____.

   （用意：表示難以接受對方條款）

4. ——18% is impossible for me to accept. That will leave no margin for profit.

   ——_____.

   （用意：說服對方降價）

5. ——To conclude the deal, I'd say a reduction of at least 25% would help.

   ——_____.

（用意：拒絕成交）

E. Role-play

Practise the conversations acoording to the situations.

• **Situation 1**

The Galaxy Exhibition Company is planning an AgroExpo that is expecting 600 exhibitors. Each need a standard pavilion(10m*10m). Decide how much space you have to reserve from the exhibition center, and negotiate the price terms with the exhibition center. With your partner, act out the Dialogue using the skills you have just learnt in this unit.

• **Situation 2**

You are an exhibitor from Australia. You are calling to hire a stand. You want to know whether you still stand a chance to have a stand near the main entrance.

You are working as a receptionist in Shanghai New International Exposition Center. Tell the exhibitor that there are some stands of his kind left.

• **Situation 3**

You are an exhibitor from Great Britain. You are calling to hire a stand. You want to the size of stand areas and the possibility of designing you own stands.

You are working as a receptionist in Shanghai New International Exposition Center. Tell the exhibitor that the size of stand areas is of average standard.

Refenence Answer

A. Specialized Terms

1. C 2. A 3. D 4. B 5. K 6. J 7. G 8. F 9. L 10 I 11. E 12. H

D. Speaking Up

1. If you consider reducing the rental rates, I'll reserve a greater amount of exhibition space.
2. Would you let us know your counter offer?
3. Your price is still out of line with the current market price.
4. If you insist on not making a discount, I can find lower prices elsewhere.
5. I'm afraid there is no room to negotiate the price.

Chapter 7
Hiring A Stand 申請展位

▌Section 1 Listening Activities

Go over the following words and expressions before listening to the tape.

summit		n.	峰會
commemorate		v.	紀念
peak period			旺季
mammoth-sized		a.	大型的
brochure		n.	小冊子
supervisor		n.	主管
scheme		n.	方案，計畫

A. Spot Dictation

Some (1) _____ take place on a regular basis, such as the (2) _____ conference and quarterly or half-yearly meetings, while others are one-off and many involve a (3) _____ set of circumstances. The latter might involve a political summit to (4) _____ or a conference to commemorate (5) _____ _____

Meeting may last from one day to a week or more. Conferences (6) _____ _____, although there is (7) _____ _____: July and August for the summer holidays and late December--- early January for Christmas and the New Year. (8) _____ _____, a timing which makes the conference business attractive to seaside resorts.

(9) _____.
The term "convention" is usually reserved for the larger meetings. (10) _____ _____, so organizations with larger membership are likely to come into being and there is the possibility of mammoth-sized conferences.

B. Multiple Choices

Directions: *In this section you will hear several Dialogues. After each Dialogue, there are some questions. Listen to the Dialogues carefully and choose the most appropriate answer to each question from the four choices marked A, B, C and D.*

● **Dialogue 1**

1. What is the relationship between the two speakers?

  A. They are nodding acquaintance.

  B. They are two people who have just met each other.

  C. They are old acquaintance.

  D. They are colleagues.

2. What is Mr. Jacob's booth number?

  A. A26.

  B. B26.

  C. A25.

  D. B25.

● **Dialogue 2**

3. What are the two speakers talking about?

  A. Something about the market.

  B. Something about computer.

  C. Something about customers.

  D. Something about TV sets.

4. What do they feel about CD-ROM?

  A. It is of no use.

  B. It is of little use.

  C. It is cheap to buy.

  D. It has great potential.

● **Dialogue 3**

5. What is on display?

A. Toys.

B. Books.

C. Foods.

D. Drinks.

6. Who is the second speaker?

   A. The sales person.

   B. A buyer for a toy company.

   C. A person who wants to buy toys for his son.

   D. The head of a toy company.

7. What toy is on display?

   A. It's a brochure.

   B. It's a new product.

   C. It's a traditional product.

   D. It's an obsolete product.

8. Why is the sales person confident in their new selection of toys?

   A. Because they have done their research.

   B. Because they have already sold a lot of toys.

   C. Because the toys are very cheap.

   D. Because the toys are very expensive.

● Dialogue 4

9. Where does this Dialogue probably take place?

   A. At the airport.

   B. Outside the exhibition hall.

   C. At an exhibition stand.

   D. At a shop.

10. What is the man interested in?

   A. The camera on display.

   B. The TV set on display.

   C. The toy on display.

   D. The machine on display.

11. The cameras are on offer, aren't they?

A. No, they aren't.

B. Yes, they are.

C. Yes, they aren't.

D. No, they are.

12. Have the cameras been exported to other countries?

A. No, they haven't.

B. Yes, they have been exported to a few countries.

C. Yes, they have been exported to western countries only.

D. Yes, they have been exported to many countries.

C. Passage Dictation

Directions: *In this section, you will hear a passage. Listen carefully and write down what you hear on the tape.*

_____

_____

_____

_____

_____

_____

_____

_____

_____

Tape script & Answers

A. Spot Dictation

Tape script:

Some (1) <u>conferences</u> take place on a regular basis, such as the (2) <u>annual</u> conference and quarterly or half-yearly meetings, while others are one-off and many involve a (3) <u>unique</u> set of circumstances. The latter might involve a political summit to (4) <u>solve a crisis</u> or a conference to commemorate (5) <u>the anniversary of a past event</u>.

Meeting may last from one day to a week or more. Conferences (6) <u>occur throughout the year</u>, although there is (7) <u>a lull in the holiday periods</u>: July and August for the summer holidays and late December--- early January for Christmas and the New Year. (8) <u>The peak periods tend to be from March to June and September to November</u>, a timing which makes the conference business attractive to seaside resorts.

(9) <u>Conferences vary in size from ten people to more than 20000 participants</u>. The term "convention" is usually reserved for the larger meetings. (10) <u>As national and international organization evolve</u>, so organizations with larger membership are likely to come into being and there is the possibility of mammoth-sized conferences.

B. Multiple Choices

Tape script:

● **Dialogue 1**

Woman:	Hi, Jacob! It's been a long time. How have you been?
Man:	Great. Customer response to our new products is strong, and we've been very busy. But we still need inexpensive quality products to meet our customers' needs. I hope I can find some at the exhibition.
Woman:	I have some products that can meet your needs.
Man:	I believe you have. I really like your last year's model.
Woman:	And I'm sure you'll be interested in our latest product this year, it's got extra functions at reasonable price.
Man:	What do you mean by extra functions?
Woman:	Why don't you drop by booth A25 and see for yourself?
Man:	Booth A25. I'll see you there.

● **Dialogue 2**

Man:	What do you think of the seminar?
Woman:	I think it is very helpful. CD-ROM definitely has great potential.
Man:	Yes, you are right. I'm totally amazed at the application of CD-ROM to multimedia computers.

Woman:	I feel the same way. But the prices must be brought down before CD-ROM really cuts into the market.
Man:	I certainly agree with you on that.
Woman:	Probably it will take five years to become popular worldwide.
Man:	I'm afraid then it will take away our customers.

● Dialogue 3

Woman:	Good afternoon, sir. Here's a brochure for you.
Man:	Good afternoon.
Woman:	May I know what application for this toy do you have in mind?
Man:	Well, I'm a buyer for a toy company. I've never seen this before. Are you sure kids will like it?
Woman:	There is always a risk, but we have done our research.
Man:	Who does your market research?
Woman:	Actually, we do it ourselves. We bring our campus and ask them questions.
Man:	So, you are confident these toys will be successful.
Woman:	Absolutely. We are so confident in our new selection of toys that we will buy them back from clients if necessary.
Man:	Let me think about it some more.
Woman:	This is a great deal. We supply a lot of stores.
Man:	Yes, it seems Good. My supervisor needs to approve this first.
Woman:	Maybe you can talk to our technical specialist if you are interested. Our company's contact is given in the brochure. Would you please leave your company's name and address with us for the further service?
Man:	Sure. Here is my business card.

● Dialogue 4

Woman:	Good morning, sir. Welcome to our exhibition counter. Here is my card.
Man:	Good morning.
Woman:	May I know what you are interested in, sir?
Man:	I'm interested in your camera.
Woman:	Good. This product is the results of our latest technology.
Man:	Do you have written materials that I can take with me?
Woman:	Certainly. Here is all the information you might need. Please take it for your reference.

Man: Thank you. Hmm, I've already seen some of the items we'd like to order.

Woman: Let me show you how to operate this camera, sir.

Man: It's not too complicated. Are they available for purchase? I'll make a comparison.

Woman: Sorry, these products are not for sale. And as far as I know, there is no one else producing these items yet.

Man: Really? But I saw them on sales in some countries.

Woman: They are our products. We have exported them in very large quantities to Many countries this year.

Man: I'm convInced that they will sell well. May I have your company's contact?

Woman: This is our company's e-mail address, Website and telephone number. If you have any question, don't hesitate to contact us. Please leave your address and telephone number for service after the sale.

Answer:

1. C 2. C 3. B 4. D 5. A 6. B 7. B 8. A 9. C 10. A 11. A 12. D

C. Passage Dictation

You should also offer a convention planner a variety of layout scheme for a specific hall. An exhibit in a hall seemingly too large for it looks awful—it carries the stigma of failure on the part of the association to attract enough exhibitors. A different layout might provide wider aisles, or conference or rest areas; or perhaps the exhibitors could be spaced out to make for a better looking, more efficient exhibit. Screens or temporary walls could be used to block off unoccupied areas. The appearance of the exhibit is important to the hotel as well as to the convention planner. It is to your interest that the exhibit looks great.

The schematics should be presented to the convention executive early enough to help prepare convention brochures.

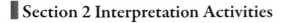

Section 2 Interpretation Activities

A. Sentecce Interpretation

1. First, find out the equivalents of the following words.

licensed	有資質的
presentation aid	演示輔助工具
distraction	容易分散注意力的東西
菸火裝置	Firework display
易燃物品	flammable substance
加強管理	control carefully

2. Read the following to your partner for him or her to put them down in Chinese or English.

1. Location preparation is made up of many points related to the specific conditions of the venue: when you get it, and what you will need it for.

2. Venue management companies should insist that their customers use licensed, insured, and reputable engineering companies to install their decorations if they are out of the ordinary.

3. If the decoration will use a large amount of electricity for huge light displays, there should be an extra electricity charge Included in the contract.

4. Most formal meetings have groups on both sides of a table, sitting in chairs and probably using presentation aids of some kind.

5. The table should be a standard height, with no distractions in the middle like plants that will stop one side seeing the other.

6. 根據安排的活動種類的不同，場館準備也將有所不同。

7. 裝飾工作大部分取決於會展管理公司，但是還有許多關鍵要點也需要有場館管理公司參與。

8. 因此，對於這些焰火裝置以及其他易燃物品應加強管理。

9. 只要服務良好，他們通常會再度光臨。

10. 在會議過程中為商務人士提供所需的服務非常重要。

B. Passage Interpretation

1. First, find out the equivalents of the following words.

accessibility	容易得到
amenities	娛樂設施
revitalization	恢復元氣
Messe	德國展覽中心
periphery	周邊地區
Frankfurt	蘭克福
Glasgow	格拉斯哥
insufficient car parking	停車場不足
congested road access.	道路擁擠
Cologne	科隆
單獨使用	used independently
按專業目標建造的	purpose-built

2. Read the following passages to yourself and render them into Chinese or English.

● **Passage 1**

At the level of the urban region there is often a debate to best location for an exhibition centre. A central site near the city centre provides the facility with Good accessibility by public transport, and access to the varied amenities of the downtown zone, Including hotels and night life, and assists with the revitalization of the inner city. Early twentieth-century Messe, such as those of Cologne and Frankfurt are in fact centrally located, but later centres are likely to have found inner city is in decay, such as in Glasgow, has it been possible to build an exhibition centre in the central area. Inner city sites may have problems with insufficient car parking and congested road access. Frequently it has been necessary to choose a site on the periphery where undeveloped land was available with Good communications and at low cost.

Your Answer

_____

_____

_____

_____

_____

_____

_____

_____

_____

● Passage 2

　　展覽在寬敞的大廳裡舉行，一個展覽中心通常有一系列的相連接的大廳組成，它們既能單獨使用，又能合併後一起使用。盛大的展覽中心可同時進行多項展覽活動。現在，大多數展覽中心是按專業目標建造的。它們有室外場地。專業的展覽場地是農業交易會，他們主要是在室外展出。展覽中心也需有提供餐飲的設施，還有辦公室。近年來，展覽中心已經開始提供會議室，因為會議常常與展覽聯繫在一起的。有時，這些會議在展覽中心附近的飯店裡召開。

Your Answer

_____

_____

_____

_____

_____

_____

_____

_____

Reference Answers

A. Sentecce Interpretation

1. 場所準備有許多要點組成，這些要點和租來的會場條件以及將把會場派做何用有關。

2. 會場管理公司應堅持要求客戶：如果他們是與眾不同的，那麼他們應聘用有資質的、保過險的、聲譽好的工程公司進行裝修。

3. 如果裝飾需要大量用電做大型的燈光展示，在合約中就會包括需要額外支付的電費。

4. 在大多數的正式會議中，人們坐在會議桌兩邊就座，可能還會使用某種演示輔助工具。

5. 桌子的高度應為標準高度，中間不能擺放諸如盆景那樣的東西，因為這些東西容易分散人們的注意力，還會擋住與會者的視線，使得彼此看不清對方。

6. Location preparation will be different depending on the kind of event you are managing.

7. Decoration is largely up to the event management company, but there are many points the venue management company will also be involved in.

8. The Use of these firework displays and other flammable substances should be controlled carefully.

9. They usually will go back again and again as long as the service is Good.

10. It is important to serve the needs of business people while they are holding their meetings.

B. Passage Interpretation

● **Passage 1**

在市區，為展覽中心選一個最佳會址常會引起爭論。靠近市中心的地方，乘公車容易到達，接近繁華商業區的各種令人愉快的環境，如飯店和夜生活，有助於恢復城市的活力。20 世紀初期的德國展覽中心，如科隆和法蘭克福的展覽中心，實際定位於市中心。但是，後來已經發現展覽中心定在已經很發達了的市內，費用太貴。只有在城內，如格拉斯哥尚有餘輝的地區，建一個展覽中心是可能的。但城內可能有停車場不足和道路擁擠的問題，有必要將展覽中心選在不太發達的周邊地區。那兒交通好，費用低。

● **Passage 2**

Exhibitions are held in large halls, and an exhibition centre usually consists of a series of linked halls which can be used either independently or in combination. Very largely exhibiton centres may host more than one event at the same time. Today most exhibition centres are purpose-built. They also have space outside. A specialist type of showground is the agricultural fair ground, which is mainly outdoor display space. Exhibition centres also require catering facilities and perhaps office space. In recent years exhibition centres have begun to provide rooms for meetings, sInce conferences often take place in association with shows. Sometimes these conferences take place in hotels which have been built nearby.

Section 3 Speaking Activities

A. Specialized Terms

Match the expressions on the left with the best Chinese equivalent on the right.

1. stand	A. 單獨設計的展台
2. booth	B. 歐式展棚
3. hire	C. 北美式展棚
4. book	D. 過道
5. modular	E. 通道
6. shell stand	F. 框架 / 骨架組合單元
7. shell module keynoter	G. 框架 / 骨架展台 (只完成框架 , 內部由購買者自己裝修的展台)
8. gangway	H. 有標準元件的
9. aisle	I. 預訂
10. north american booth	J. 租用
11. european shell scheme	K. 展棚
12. individual designed stand	L. 展台

B. Sample Conversation

Listen and read aloud.

Situation: Shirley White is calling to enquire about reserving a exhibit stand at the 22nd World Nursing Congress.

A: Hello, Information Department of International Exhibition & Convention Center. This is Hazel Brown speaking. Can I help you?

B: This is Shirley White speaking. I'm calling to make sure the arrangement when I am attending the 22nd World Nursing Congress.

A: Okay, Ms. White. We are ready to provide any convenience.

B: Thanks. I'm wondering if you can help me reserve a room from 23rd, the day before the congress until 28th, the last day of the congress.

A: Yes. You could have two choices: Hotel Marriott with a room rate of $100 and Radisson SAS Royal hotel of $120 per day.

B: Which one is nearer to the Congress Center?

A: I am afraid Radisson is nearer.

B: Then I'd like to take it. Besides, is there still any stand available for the exhibition during the Congress?

A: Let me check. Yes. We do have several stands left but quite far away from the entrance.

B: That is not important. How much is it if I hire a stand for one day to do some consulting and advertising for my nursing agency?

A: We give a 10% discount for the inner stands, i.e., $120 dollars per day.

B: Done. By the way, what's the weather like in Copenhagen?

A: It is the best season now in Copenhagen, neither too hot nor too cold. You should spare some time to do sightseeing when you're here.

B: Sure. Thank you for you help.

C. Functional Expressions

Read aloud and practice with your partner.

Talking about the booth size	Response
Can you explain to me the options of stands first?	We offer package stand and raw space.
What is the area for raw space?	The minimum area for one raw space indoor is twenty-seven square meters.
Are there any different sizes of booths?	Yes, there are two different sizes.
How large is the standard booth?	It's nine feet by ten feet.

Enquiring about booth price	Response
How much do you charge for the stands and raw space respectively?	The package stands cost at least 24,550 Yuan RMB per unit, equivalent to about 3,000 US dollars.
Does the price of the show Include meals?	Yes, the cost of meals is Included.

What is Included in the price?	It covers the food and accommodations and the cost of a booth in the corner.
Are there any different costs for the package stands?	Yes. Costs vary with the different locations of the stand.
Do you cheaper ones?	Then you may choose corner stands.
What is least expensive booth you have?	We have a few spaces left in the back for 12,000 Yuan RMB.

Choosing booths locations

If the price is right, I'll take the booth in the center.

I will set up in the center if the price is reasonable.

If it doesn't cost too much I will choose the center location.

Bargaining for booth rentals	Response
Can you make a cut rate for me?	Sorry to say that we can't, but we can Increase the dimension of your space a little without Incurring extra fee.
Can you lower the price for the center booth?	I cannot lower the price for you, but I can make your space a little bit bigger.
Is it possible to reduce the price?	I can Increase the size of the spot, but I can't decrease the price.
What are the best terms of booth price?	I will enlarge your spot a little, but I will not drop the price.

D. Speaking Up

Render the following into English by using as many language skills learnt as possible.

1. 請問我的展位在哪裡？
2. 這是會場佈置圖。我們現在的位置是服務台，您的展位在這。
3. 我只想確定以下所有東西都已到位，並且沒有問題。
4. 我們一定要在下午一點之前佈置好。
5. 我現在可以去看一看月台和貨物嗎？

E. Role-play

Practise the conversation in English.

● **Part 1**

    A： 請問一個標準攤位的費用是多少？

    B： 每個標準攤位是 1,800 美元。

    A： 我並不需要整個攤位，只要一半就夠了。

    B： 我剛好知道有另一家公司想要合用攤位。

    A： 太好了。如果合用一個攤位的話，該付多少錢？

    B： 你預付一半的費用。

    A： 你能給我一些這個公司的資料嗎？

    B： 我查到後再打電話給你，可以嗎？

    A： 請儘快告訴我。

● **Part 2**

● **Situation 1**

    C. You are an exhibitor from Australia. You are calling to hire a stand. You want to know whether you still stand a chance to have a stand near the main entrance.

    D. You are working as a receptionist in Shanghai New International Exposition Center. Tell the exhibitor that there are some stands of his kind left.

● **Situation 2**

    C. You are an exhibitor from Great Britain. You are calling to hire a stand. You want to the size of stand areas and the possibility of designing you own stands.

    D. You are working as a receptionist in Shanghai New International Exposition Center. Tell the exhibitor that the size of stand areas is of average standard.

Reference Answers

A. Specialized Terms

1. l 2. k 3. j 4. i 5. h 6. g 7. f 8. e 9. d 10. c 11. b 12. a

D. Speaking Up

1. Could you tell me where I can find my booth?
2. Here's a map of the exhibition hall, and here we are at the service desk. It is your booth.
3. I just want to be sure that everything is here and in working condition.
4. We really need to set up before 1:00 in the afternoon.
5. Do you think I could check on my booth and my Goods now?

Chapter 8
Personal Sales Calls 銷售拜訪（電話）

▎Section 1 Listening Activities

Go over the following words and expressions before listening to the tape.

1 deferment		n.	遷延，延期，暫緩
2. IC chips		v.	智慧晶片
3. Incorporate		n.	促進
4. mascot			吉祥物
5.specs		n.	規格
6 counterfeit		v.	偽造，假冒
7 miniature		adj.	微型的
8 authenticate		v.	鑒別

A. Spot Dictation

Street promotions require that you (1) _____ take your message to the street. This marketing (2) _____ may Include the handing out of flyers by a clown in a (3) _____ area, the appearance of a celebrity (4) _____ , contests, or other promotional activities designed to (5) _____ to your event. (6) _____ (handing out flyers), make certain that this is allowed by (7) _____. You certainly don't want to generate negative publicity by having the clown arrested for causing a disturbance. (8) _____. Schedule the celebrity to Include radio and television interviews, appearances at a local children's hospital or other public facility, and ceremonial events with local, state, provIncial, or federal leaders. (9) __ _____ _ . Contests and other promotional events also require analysis to ensure that they are within the bounds of the local code and that they are appropriate for your event. (10) _____ .

B. Multiple Choices

Directions: *In this section you will hear several Dialogues. After each Dialogue, there are some questions. Listen to the Dialogue carefully and choose the most appropriate answer to each question from the four choices marked A, B, C and D.*

• **Dialogue 1**

1.According to the Dialogue, when can the exhibitors begin to decorate their booths?

On the night just before the exhibition opens.

One day in advance of the exhibition.

Two days in advance of the exhibition.

Three days in advance of the exhibition.

2. What if the decorating team needs additional electric power?

Ask help from the exhibition coordinator.

Ask help at the exhibition information desk.

Ask help from the exhibition manager.

Ask help from the electrician present at the venue.

3. Which one of the following statements is not true according to the Dialogue?

The decorating team must leave the exhibition hall before 8:30 p.m.

The organizer is asking that no one change his or her booth number.

Most of our customers take semi-finished articles to the exhibition hall.

No deferment is permitted if the exhibitor cannot finish decorating in time.

• **Dialogue 2.**

4. How long has the exhibitor been waiting for the Goods rented?

A. Half an hour.

B. One hour.

C. One and a half hour.

D. Two hours.

5. What items does the exhibitor want to rent?

A. One telephone and one chairs.

B. One flowers and one icebox.

C. One telephone and one how box.

D. One telephone and one icebox.

6. What is the probable cause for the delay?

A. The service person mistakes the booth number.

B. The service person is busy and forgets that.

C. The venue clerk did not arrange it.

D. The venue clerk mistakes the booth number.

● Dialogue 3.

7. What does Miss Smith think of Mr. Wang's exhibition?

A. Just so so.

B. Better than the previous one.

C. Nice.

D. Best of all she has visited.

8. What does Mr. Wang wish Miss Smith to have a look at?

A. The price list.

B. The new products.

C. Some samples.

D. Both a and C.

9. What does Miss Smith focus on when it comes to making a purchase?

A. Quality and design of products.

B. Quality and price of products.

C. Design and price of products.

D. New products.

● Dialogue 4.

10. Before filling in the contract, what did the two sides do ?

A. Check the commodity name and specs.

B. Check unit price and sum total of the commodity.

C. Check the items of the contract.

D. Check the shipment deadline.

11. What does Miss Smith insist?

    A. The shipment should be finished by the end of May.

    B. The shipment should be finished by April 30.

    C. The shipment should be finished by May 1.

    D. The shipment should be finished by the end of March.

12. Which one of the following is not true according to the Dialogue?

    A. The two sides have reached an agreement on price.

    B. It is the commodity unit price but not sum total that is necessary in the contract.

    C. Miss Smith keeps the original and two photocopies.

    D. The two sides have a drink to celebrate after signing the contract.

C. Passage Dictation

Directions: *In this section, you will hear a passage. Listen carefully and write down what you hear on the tape.*

_____

_____

_____

_____

_____

_____

_____

_____

_____

_____

Tape script & Answers:

A. Spot Dictation

    Street promotions require that you (1) <u>literally</u> take your message to the street. This marketing (2) <u>activity</u> may Include the handing out of flyers by a clown in a

(3) <u>high-traffic</u> area, the appearance of a celebrity (4) <u>at a local mall</u>, contests, or other promotional activities designed to (5) <u>draw high visibility to your event.</u> (6) Before <u>leafleting</u> (handing out flyers), make certain that this is allowed by (7) <u>local code</u>. You certainly don't want to generate negative publicity by having the clown arrested for causing a disturbance. (8) <u>A celebrity appearance can help generate significant publicity if it is handled properly.</u> Schedule the celebrity to Include radio and television interviews, appearances at a local children's hospital or other public facility, and ceremonial events with local, state, provIncial, or federal leaders. (9) <u>At each appearance make certain that the celebrity is well informed about the event and articulates your event message in a consistent manner.</u> Contests and other promotional events also require analysis to ensure that they are within the bounds of the local code and that they are appropriate for your event. (10) <u>For instance, selling raffle tickets at a nonprofit event may require that you file legal forms.</u>

B. Multiple Choices

● **Dialogue 1**

Tape script:

Man:	When can I come to decorate our booth?
Woman:	As regulated, your decoration team can begin its work two days before the exhibition, but it must leave the exhibition hall before 8:30 p.m. If the team needs additional electric power and water or needs some tools, it should register at the exhibition information desk. This year, the organizer is asking that no one change his or her booth number.
Man:	I cannot finish decorating the booth in two days. What shall I do?
Woman:	Most of our customers do the original decorating beforehand, and take semi-finished articles in, installing them. It can save a lot of time. Also, the night before the exhibition, if you cannot finish the work, you can apply for deferment. But you should pay an additional fee for that.
Man:	OK, thank you.

● **Dialogue 2.**

Tape script:

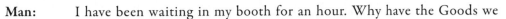

Man: I have been waiting in my booth for an hour. Why have the Goods we rented not arrived yet?

Woman: Sorry, Mr. Wang. Maybe the service person in the exhibition hall got your booth number wrong. I will arrange for them to send you the Goods immediately.

Man: I'm on a tight schedule. The builders are leaving soon.

Woman: I'm so sorry about that. If your builders and designers are about to leave, we will take responsibility for installing the telephone and the icebox for you.

Man: OK.

● **Dialogue 3.**

Tape script:

Man: Good morning, Miss Smith.

Woman: Morning, Mr. Wang. Glad to meet you again. How's everything?

Man: Fine. What do you think of our exhibition this time?

Woman: Very nice. I think you have learned a lot from the previous exhibition.

Man: Yes. Today I have a price list and samples of our new products here. I hope you can have a look.

Woman: Do you have the all samples of the products here?

Man: No, just some of them. If you can visit our company some day, there are samples of all our products.

Woman: Sure, I am willing to do that.

Man: I can show you most of our products with PowerPoint.

Woman: I'm very impressed by your products, and I'd be glad to make a purchase. Let me think about it carefully. If the quality of the cotton is as Good as that of the samples, and the price is reasonable, I plan to order products from your company.

Man: I can assure you of the quality. As for the price, you will find it is also very attractive.

Woman: Let me think it over.

● **Dialogue 4.**

Tape script:

Man:	Miss Smith, the two sides have reached an agreement on price. Should we look at the items of the contract again?
Woman:	OK.
Man:	Let's begin with the name, specs, amount, unit price and sum total of the commodity.
	(After checking)
Man:	Any other questions?
Woman:	No, but I must insist that shipment should be finished by the end of April and I cannot accept a delay for any reason.
Man:	OK.
Woman:	Fine. Let's fill in the contract with the items we just talked about.
Man:	(After finishing filling in the contract) Should I sign right now?
Woman:	Fine. Here you are.
Man:	You keep the original and two photocopies.
Woman:	Thank you. I'm so glad that we made this deal and established a business relationship with you.
Man:	Yes. I hope we can extend our cooperation after this. Let's have a drink to celebrate!
Woman:	Good idea.

Answers:

1.C 2. B 3. D 4. B 5. D 6. A 7. C 8.D 9. B 10. C 11.B 12. B

C. Passage Dictation

Tape script:

EXPO 2005 Aichi tickets go on sale September 25, 2003. They Include special discount admission tickets that take into account advance purchase, day of the week and time of visit, repeat and group visits, to encourage the whole world to visit EXPO 2005 Aichi. First-term advance purchase tickets will go on sale at a 20% discount on September 25, 2003, a year and a half before the opening of the EXPO. In another first for world expos, IC chips will be Incorporated in the ticket design that features the official EXPO mascots Morizo and Kiccoro. A miniature 0.4mm chip will be embedded in each entry ticket to prevent counterfeiting. Each ticket will have a unique identification code (ID number), which can be authenticated simply by placing the ticket over a reader. The IC chip is expected to broaden the range of services, Including identification of ticket type, to be made available to visitors.

Section 2 Interpretation Activities

A. Sentence Interpretation

1. First, find out the equivalents of the following words.

public relation breakthrough competitive marketing force 潛在群體 行銷策略	

2. Read the following to your partner for him or her to put them down in Chinese or English.

1. There is no question that the development of the Internet has become the most important communication and marketing media breakthrough sInce the printing press in the mid-fifteenth century.

2. It has been shown that those events that are close to inexpensive, safe public transportation or those events that feature closed-in reasonably priced parking will attract more guests than those that do not offer these amenities.

3. Advertising is what you say about your event, whereas public relation is what others are saying about your event.

4. In most cases, event managers use marketing forces such as advertising, public relations, promotion, advertising specialties, stunts, and other techniques to promote individual events.

5. The Internet will continue to drive the development of the global event management industry. You must use this dynamic technology quickly and accurately to ensure that your event remains competitive throughout the twenty-first century.

6. 在會展活動業中，目標市場這個術語的含義主要是指參加某一特定活動的潛在群體。

7. 選擇機場旅館，是因為這一場所飛進飛出的航班使與會者能夠花費最少的旅行時間，高效地完成工作。

8. 每一個會展活動都有其獨特性，即使並非如此，行銷人員也要努力把它表現成這樣。

9. 無論一項會展活動的性質如何，其成功與否都取決於採用何種行銷策略來吸引消費者。

10. 作為會展活動行銷的一個重要組成部分，市場調研和分析有助於行銷人士確定其目標市場的態度、期望及需求。

B. Passage Interpretation

1. First, find out the equivalents of the following words.

cyber	
brochureware	
static	
show-biz	
utilitarian	
brand recognition	
運營成本	
合理的活動價位	
市場競爭分析	

2. Read the following passages to yourself and render them into Chinese or English.

● Passage 1

   Today, after experiencing five consistent years of cyber growth, event marketing specialists are speaking about second and third generations of Web sites. The first and least developed type of Web site is brochureware. Web sites of this type are static and contain basic information about an organization, Including its address and services. The site reflects a paper brochure placed on the Web. The second group of Web sites is known as show-biz. These sites try to amuse visitors through interactive features, flashing pictures, news reports, or press reviews. The last and most developed type of Web sites are called utilitarian. These sites offer viewers a unique and balanced interactive service that is both highly informative and helpful in building brand recognition and loyalty.

Your Answer

_____

_____

_____

_____

_____

_____

_____

_____

● **Passage 2**

　　市場調研能幫你確定價格。市場調研的部分內容是進行市場競爭分析，分析其他提供相似活動的組織。最初，你也許會認為自己的會展活動獨一無二。但是，當你與潛在的購票者或客人溝通時，你會吃驚地發現他們認為你的活動與許多活動是相近的。因此，你必須仔細一地列出所有競爭者的活動以及它們的價格，以幫助你確定一個合理的活動價位。一般來說，有兩個因素決定價格：運營成本和市場競爭。

Your Answer

_____

_____

_____

_____

_____

_____

_____

_____

Reference Answer

A. Sentence Interpretation

1.

public relation	公共關係
breakthrough	突破
competitive	有競爭力的
marketing force	行銷方式
潛在群體	potential group
行銷策略	marketing strategy

2.

1. 毫無疑問，自十五世紀中葉印刷媒體發展以來，互聯網的發展已經成為在溝通和行銷媒介方面最重要的突破。

2. 據認為，那些毗鄰價廉且安全的公共交通工具的會展活動，以及那些擁有封閉和價格合理的停車場所的活動，比那些無法提供以上便利措施的活動，更加吸引消費者。

3. 廣告是你自己對於會展活動的宣傳，而公共關係是他人對於活動的看法。

4. 在大多數情況下，會展活動經理人採用廣告、公關、促銷、廣告宣傳品、驚險表演等行銷方式來推廣活動。

5. 互聯網將繼續推動全球活動管理業的發展。你必須迅速準確地應用這種動態發展的技術，以使你的活動在整個二十一世紀始終保持競爭力。

6. The term "target market" refers, in the main, to the people who would be coming to a particular event in the event industry.

7. Airport hotels are chosen because the fly-in fly-out design of the location enables the attendees to get the work done with the minimum travel time.

8. Every event is unique. Even if this may not be the case, at least event marketers need to endeavor to present it as such.

9. Regardless of the nature of the event, its success largely depends on what marketing strategies are adopted to attract consumers.

10. As a key component of event marketing, market research and analysis helps the marketer to determine the attitudes, expectations and needs of the target market.

B. Passage Interpretation

1.

cyber	電腦
brochureware	宣傳冊式網頁
static	靜態的
show-biz	娛樂新聞式網頁
utilitarian	專用型網頁
brand recognition	創造品牌認知度
運營成本	the cost of doing business
合理的活動價位	the appropriate price for your event.
市場競爭分析	competitive analysis study

2.

● Passage 1

如今，在經歷了連續五年的電腦應用增長之後，會展活動行銷專家們正在探討第二代和第三代網頁。最早的也是最不先進的網頁是宣傳冊式網頁。這種類型的網頁是靜態的，只包含一個組織的基本資訊，如位址和服務專案。它就像把一個紙制的宣傳冊放在網上。第二種網頁是娛樂新聞式網頁，它採用互動、動畫、新聞報導、媒體評論的方式來愉悅訪問者。最後的也是最發達的網頁類型是專用型網頁。它為訪問者提供一種獨特而穩定的互動式服務，其中既包含大量資訊，又有利於創造品牌認知度和忠誠度。

● Passage 2

Market research will help you determine price. Part of this market research will Include conducting a competitive analysis study of other organizations offering similar event products. You may initially believe that your product is uniquely different from every other event. However, when interview potential ticket buyers or guests you may be surprised to learn that they consider your event similar to many others. Therefore, you must carefully list all competing events and the prices being charged to help you determine the appropriate price for your event. Typically, two factors determine price, i.e., the cost of doing business and the marketplace competition.

Section 3 Speaking Activities

A. Specialized Terms

Match the expressions on the left with the best Chinese equivalent on the right.

1. personal sales call	A. 集中銷售
2. trade show selling	B. 未經預約的拜訪（或電話）
3. familiarization tour	C. 現場視察
4. telephone sales call follow-up	D. 展會銷售
5. cold call	E. 開放性問題
6. sales blitzes	F. 電話銷售後續聯繫
7. screening prospects	G. 篩選潛在客戶
8. telemarketing	H. 個別拜訪（電話）銷售
9. open-ended question	I. 電話推銷
10. destination marketing	J. 目的地銷售

B. Sample Conversation

Listen and read aloud.

Situation: Su-Hui, sales clerk of the Claude Convention Center, is paying a personal sales call to a foreign-funded electronic enterprise in China. She is talking face to face with a prospect about convention sales.

Su-Hui: Good morning, Mr. Hilton. How is everything?

Hilton: Couldn't be better. Thanks. And you?

Su-Hui: Me too. Is any event you are planning for next year?

Hilton: Yes, we'll be having a new series of training sessions next year. Are you able to serve this event in your center?

Su-Hui: I'm delighted if our convention center can be of service to you. Now let me show you the floor plans and the map of the facilities. You can see how it can serve your future needs. I believe you would be very interested.

Hilton: I remember you have had new meeting facilities, right?

Su-Hui: Yes, you're right, Mr. Hilton. We are now building a specially-designed conference hall. It will open in 3 months' time. We'll be honored if we could come as our distinguished guest to a special opening reception and tour the weekend of October 21 to October 22.

Hilton: Thank you. I'd love to.

Su-Hui: Is it that each department in your company is to conduct its own training meetings? Could you tell me the size of the training party?

Hilton: We have 30 trainees.

Su-Hui: I'm sure I'll find our smaller multimedia rooms ideally meeting your needs.

Hilton: You will not charge us for audio-visual equipment, will you?

Su-Hui: If you are sure you could book 400 room nights, we can also let you have your opening reception free of charge.

Hilton: My last meeting was totally spoiled (毀壞了) by those two Incompetents on my staff who are supposed to handle all details and they made sure that all points were covered.

Su-Hui: No worry, sir. We can solve your problem. We have just hired three experienced assistant convention Managers. They would be happy to take up these service details for you.

Hilton: That would be Good. I shall consult with the general Manager about this. I'll see you to touch the details once we've decided.

Su-Hui: Thank you, Mr. Hilton. We look forward to seeing you soon again.

C. Functional Expressions

Read aloud and practice with your partner.

- **Opening the sales call**

  Good afternoon, Mr. Hilton. I'm Su-Hui from the Claude International Convention Center, Shanghai.

  I've heard so much about what your firm has been doing in the area of printer technology and application. And I'm eager to hearing more about your innovation.

  Would you be interested in learning how other associations used one of our theme parties to Increase attendance?

  May I show you a few examples of our state-of-the –art audiovisual system?

- **Getting prospect involvement**

  Where did you have your Incentive meeting?

  How many training meetings do you stage each month?

  What is your average attendance at your annual convention?

Why do you think last year's meeting was so successful?

What are the essential elements to you in selecting a meeting site?

● **Closing the sales call**

Don't you think our audiovisual equipment will greatly enhance your training sessions?

Don't you think our ballroom would make an elegant setting for your awards banquet?

Don't you find our golf course to be one of the finest in the state?

May I reserve space on a definite basis?

D. Speaking Up

Render the following into Chinese by using as many language skills learnt as possible.

1. We have a health club and spa so that your trainees can relax and unwind after a day of intensive educational meetings.

2. Every room has a desk so that your meeting attendees will have plenty of room to review and work on handouts they receive during the daily meeting sessions.

3. You may have easy access to secretarial service because PC computer stations, facsimile and copiers are available in our business center.

4. The attendees can expect to cut check-in time because we have simplified checking in program: "Zip-In Check-In".

5. VIPs will be identified easily by our staff because the VIPs are given "Gold Pins" by our convention center.

E. Role-play

Practise the conversations acoording to the situations.

● **Situation 1**

A major U.S. ABC Computer Corporation is calling the Shanghai Claude Hotel to get some information about the group prices of rooms and seasonal prices of rooms. In pairs, try the Dialogue using your real names. One person will be the assistant manager for ABC Computer Corporation. The other person will be the sales manager for the Shanghai Claude Hotel.

• Situation 2

Su-Hui was hired as a sales trainee a year ago, and was promoted to salesman after only six months. She has made Good, but not outstanding, progress, meeting her sales quota by only slim margins. She is now beginning her second year of personal selling and wants to expand her current prospect list by making cold calls. Try to give Su-Hui some suggestions about the skills of making cold calls. One person plays the role of Su-Hui. The other is you.

Reference Answer

A. Specialized Terms

1 H 2 D 3 C 4 F 5 B 6 A 7 G 8 I 9 E 10 J

Chapter 9
Hiring People and Loaning Properties 租借物品 / 租用人員

▌Section 1 Listening Activities

Go over the following words and expressions before listening to the tape.

1 billboard		n.	佈告板，看板
2 fragile		A.	易碎的，脆的
3 horologe		n.	鐘錶
4 foster		A.	撫育，培養，鼓勵
5 FPA	平安險		
6.WPA	水漬險		
7.breakage risk	破碎險		
8.all risk	一切險		

A. Spot Dictation

Human Resources Startup Checklist

—Have you prepared and determined　(1)＿＿＿＿＿＿＿ and specifications for each position that must be filled?

—Have you prepared full job (2)＿＿＿＿＿ for key positions in the organization?

—Do you know how to find the people you need to fill these positions?

—What (3).＿＿＿＿＿ employees will be hired in the event of growth?

—Have you (4).＿＿＿＿＿＿ the practices and methods you will use to hire/fire employees? Are they legal?

—Are you (5)＿＿＿＿＿ the Employment Standards Code?

—Have you established policies on wages and salaries, (6)＿＿＿＿＿

when raises are given, how often employees are paid, how much vacation is earned and when taken?

—Have you (7)_____ employee benefits, Including pensions, group insurance, profit-sharing, etc.?

—(8)_____

_____

— Do you have the skills to lead and motivate your employees?

—(9)_____

_____

—Can you communicate effectively with employees? If not, can you develop this skill?

(10)_____

B. Multiple Choices

Directions: *In this section you will hear several Dialogues. After each Dialogue, there are some questions. Listen to the Dialogues carefully and choose the most appropriate answer to each question from the four choices marked A, B, C and D.*

● Dialogue 1

1. How long is the history of the International Household Utensil Exhibition?

    A. 30 years.

    B. 22 years.

    C. 32 years.

    D. 20 years.

2. What is this exhibition famous for?

    A. The large numbers of professional buyers

    B. The high quality of service

    C. The long history

    D. The highly efficient in signing contracts

3. What is the deadline of exhibition registration?

    A. May 17th.

    B. March 17th.

    C. March 18th.

D. May 18th.

●**Dialogue 2**

4. Why does the exhibitor want to know about the advertising arrangements?

A. For saving money.

B. For better preparation.

C. For saving time.

D. For booth decorating.

5. Which one of the following is not Included in the advertising arrangements?

A. A brochure of all the participants and sponsors.

B. A full page advertisement in International Business.

C. Outdoor advertising.

D. A participant's index.

6. In terms of outdoor advertising, which one of the following is true?

A. The organizer do not provide outdoor advertisements.

B. Billboards are not Included in the outdoor advertising.

C. Outdoor advertisements will charge extra fee.

D. Outdoor advertising has a better effect than indoor advertising.

●**Dialogue 3**

7 .Where will this exhibition be held?

A. United Kingdom.

B. United states.

C. France.

D. China.

8. Whose needs does the exhibition mainly meet?

A. American and Mexican clients'.

B. African and American clients'.

C. African and Mexican clients'.

D. American and Canadian clients'.

9. How much does every standard booth cost?

A. About RMB 25000 yuan.

B. About RMB 20000 yuan.

C. About RMB 2500 yuan.

D. About RMB 2000 yuan.

• Dialogue 4

10. Which one of the following is not Included in the basic transport risks?

A. Particular risks.

B. F.P.A..

C. W.P.A.

D. All risks.

11. What kind of risk does war risk belong to?

A. Basic risk.

B. All risks.

C. W.P.A.

D. Additional risk.

12. Why does Mr. Martin suggest the exhibitor insure their display items against breakage?

A. Its premium rate is relatively low.

B. It is a kind of normal insurance.

C. The items are easy to be broken.

D. The items are porcelain wares.

C. Passage Dictation

Directions: *In this section, you will hear a passage. Listen carefully and write down what you hear on the tape.*

_____

_____

_____

_____

_____

_____

_____
_____
_____
_____

Tape script & Answers:

A. Spot Dictation

Tape script:

Human Resources Startup Checklist

—Have you prepared and determined (1) <u>qualifications</u> and specifications for each position that must be filled?

—Have you prepared full job (2) <u>descriptions</u> for key positions in the organization?

—Do you know how to find the people you need to fill these positions?

—What (3) <u>additional</u> employees will be hired in the event of growth?

—Have you (4) <u>given thought to</u> the practices and methods you will use to hire/fire employees? Are they legal?

—Are you (5) <u>familiar with</u> the Employment Standards Code?

—Have you established policies on wages and salaries, (6) <u>such as but not limited to</u>: when raises are given, how often employees are paid, how much vacation is earned and when taken?

—Have you (7) <u>made decisions on</u> employee benefits, Including pensions, group insurance, profit-sharing, etc.?

—(8) <u>Have you developed a method for evaluating your employees' performance?</u>

—Do you have the skills to lead and motivate your employees?

—(9) <u>Have you established a corporate philosophy that is basic enough for your employees to follow?</u>

—Can you communicate effectively with employees? If not, can you develop this skill?

(10) <u>Are the employees you need available at this location?</u>

B. Multiple Choices

Tape script:

• **Dialogue 1**

Man: I want to know more about the International Household Utensil Exhibition.

Woman: It is an exhibition with a 32-year history, catering to clients from South Africa and Mexico. Over the past 32 years, the exhibition has been well known for its high efficiency in signing contracts.

Man: We want to know about the deMan:ds of the outside world so we can take advantage of market in the future.

Woman: Participating in the exhibition can be a Good beginning of helping you to get acquainted with the profession and make some new friends.

Man: Yes, thank you. Ms. Brown.

Woman: In addition, the deadline for registration is March 17th.

Man: I see. We will contact you as soon as possible. Thanks again.

• **Dialogue 2**

Man: Miss Green, I want to know the advertising arrangements for this exhibition, so we can get prepared accordingly.

Woman: This year we will provide a full page advertisement in International Business. Furthermore, we will also work out a brochure covering all the participants and a participants index.

Man: How about the outdoor advertisement?

Woman: For outdoor advertising, we will prepare a large-scale balloon, color flags, billboards, and banners, etc., but outdoor advertisements will be an additional charge.

• **Dialogue 3**

Woman: Organizing Committee of the International Household Utensil Exhibition. How may I help you?

Man: Yes. My name is John Li. I'm from China Daming Utensil Company. We have seen information about the International Household Utensil Exhibition and we'd like to get some details about it.

Woman: The exhibition will be held from May 17th to May 23rd in Miami. It mainly caters to clients in the Mexican and African markets. It has been held for 32 years and we have been doing quite successfully.

Man: Thank you for giving me this information. What about the expenses of taking part in this exhibition?

Woman: The price of every standard booth is $2500.

Man: If we want to participate, what should we do?

Woman: You must fill in a registration form and send us the fee as soon as possible.

Man: Can we book a booth now?

Woman: Yes, you can. There are some booths left.

Man: That's fine, thank you! Please reserve a booth for us. We will contact you as soon as possible.

Woman: OK, I'm glad to help you. Could you let me know how I can contact you if you don't mind?

Man: Sure. My phone number is 86-471-68826611.

● **Dialogue 4**

Woman: Mr. Martin, could you explain the insurance in greater detail? This is the first time that our company will be taking part in an international exhibition.

Man: OK. Generally speaking, according to China Safety Insurance Company, transport insurance Includes basic risks and additional risks. Basic risks consist of F.P.A., W.P.A. and all risks. The additional risks refer to other particular risks.

Woman: What are particular risks? Could you give me an example?

Man: War Risk for example, is a particular risk. Recently, due to the war in Iraq, Many companies stopped insurance against war. In Many regions, the premium rate has Increased 14 to 15 times.

Woman: Mr. Martin, What risks should be covered in your opinion?

Man: To save money, I suggest your company cover Breakage Risk.

Woman: Why should we insure against that?

Man:	Considering that Many of your company's display items are made of glass, which is fragile. Breakage risk is suitable for your products. You should consider other insurance, too.
Woman:	Oh, I see.
Man:	Here is a chart of the coverage of risks and premium rates of our company. You can have a look.
Woman:	Thank you, Mr. Martin.
Man:	You are welcome.

Answers:

1.C 2. D 3. B 4. B 5. A 6. C 7.B 8.C 9. B 10. A 11.D 12. C

C. Passage Dictation

Tape script:

China is experiencing fast development and Chinese market, a market with boundless potentials, and is maturing, especially after China's entry into the WTO when customs duties are lowered and trade policies are more open. Under this background, 2004 China International Horologe Exhibition, aiming at fostering and exploiting horologe market, will be staged. It will construct a platform for every exhibitor from both home and abroad to boost your business and offer communication and Dialogue opportunities for manufacturers, importers, dealers and retailers.

Beijing is the capital of China, hub of fashion, center of mass media, and definitely your first choice to promote your brand. Here, "Watches Wonders " will be presented within the context of 2004 China International Horologe Exhibition, when Beijing will become the only destination for Chinese horology dealers and retailers.

2004 China International Horologe Exhibition, an event with endless business opportunities, will bridge you to endless success.

Section 2 Interpretation Activities

A. Sentence Interpretation

1. First, find out the equivalents of the following words.

prioritize	分出輕重緩急
coordinator	管理協調人員
uniform colors	有特定顏色的制服
theming some meal	主題化餐飲
常常談論的一個問題	frequently discussed issues
非常重要	count
想客人之所想	guest obsesse

2. Read the following to your partner for him or her to put them down in Chinese or English.

1. There are so many things you should bear in mind, so to prioritize your activities, check for any last minute changes, notes left for you, correspondence, phone messages or e-mails.

2. A check can be made of arrangements between coordinator and staff to deal with any final requests or changes to the booked details.

3. Staff is easy to identify by uniform colors or with visible ID that can be worn around the neck.

4. One thing that can't follow you around is the deliveries of supplies.

5. There is a trend towards theming some meals during events, which combines entertainment with Good food and drink.

6. 關於會議管理常常談論的一個問題是，銷售人員在服務過程中到底應該做些什麼。

7. 展會的工作人員提供服務，參展商或與會者享受服務。兩者之間，後者對展會的期望如何是非常重要的。

8. 我們要使我們的員工的服務比客人期望的要好，讓員工想客人之所想。

9. 隨著準備工作的進一步就緒，各種各樣的物品將被運送到位。

10. 展覽會和展銷會成功的一點是它能吸引足夠多的參展商來滿足參觀者的需要，同時能夠吸引足夠多的參觀者來滿足參展商的目的。

B. Passage Interpretation

1. First, find out the equivalents of the following words.

logistics	物流業務
distributed	分送
deadlines	最後日期
central arrival point	集中收貨區
flow of crew around the venue	工作人員在展館的流動
投影設備	video projection
調試設備	test their material
音箱效果	sound reinforcement
電腦文本	computer-generated text
構圖	graphics
圖像轉換	transfer of pictures

2. Read the following passages to yourself and render them into Chinese or English.

● **Passage 1**

Logistics is the discipline of planning and organizing the flow of Goods, equipment and people. Logistics Includes ticketing and enquiries, arrival and departure of visitors as well as the flow of crew around the venue. Within logistics, the preparation, opening and running of an event depends on getting all the elements to the right place in time for a range of deadlines. This can be a complicated process and individual staff and departments will be expected to work with each other to get their own list of requirements prepared. And when events are being run, the convention and exhibition organizer should make sure that everything goes smoothly. Supplies can be ordered and delivery checked, usually at the central arrival point, and the supplies distributed as required to the places where they are needed.

Your Answer

_____

_____

_____

_____

_____
_____
_____
_____
_____

● Passage 2

　　技術支援是基本的服務內容。會展中心要能提供越來越複雜的技術服務。許多客戶自己設計演示軟體，要求有相應的技術支援。在會展中心有各種各樣的投影設備，一般與其他媒體結合使用。多媒體包括放像、電腦文本和構圖、數碼相機圖像轉換、在演示中增加音像效果。另一個技術方面的問題，是音響以及音響的放大。除了最小型的活動之外，都會有這方面的要求。為保證所需設備到位，場地管理方和技術人員應該要求演講者至少在活動開始一周前到場調試設備。

Your Answer

_____
_____
_____
_____
_____
_____
_____
_____
_____

Reference Answers

1.　你有那麼多的事情要記，應該分出輕重緩急，應該注意最新的一些變化，留意給你的便條、信函、電話、留言和電子郵件等。
2.　檢查一下管理協調人員與員工的工作安排，處理所有最後的報名和變更情況。
3.　所有員工穿有特定顏色的制服，胸前掛有身份證件，易於辨認。

4. 貨物送達後，不可能你在哪裡，就在哪裡收貨。

5. 現在，活動期間的用餐流行一種主題化餐飲，這是一種美味佳餚與娛樂相結合的活動。

6. One of the frequently discussed issues in convention management is the extent to which the salesperson should be involved in the servicing process.

7. It is the exhibitor or the attendee who is receiving the service, not the convention and exhibition staff who is delivering it, whose expectations count.

8. We will empower our staff to exceed out guests' expectations and to become guest obsessed.

9. Various things will be delivered as preparations progress.

10. Exhibitions and trade fairs usually succeed because they attract enough visitors to satisfy the exhibitors and enough exhibitors to satisfy the visitors.

B. Passage Interpretation

• Passage 1

　　物流業務是指計畫並組織物品、設備與人員的流動。物流業務包括票務、問詢，參觀者的接送和工作人員在展館的流動。就物流而言，一項活動的準備、開幕和運轉要求所有相關因素在一定的時間內到位。這是一個非常複雜的過程。每一個個人和部門要通力合作並按照各自的工作要求做好準備。一旦活動開始，會展組織者要保證萬無一失。貨物的預定與驗收一般在集中收貨區進行。從那裡，將貨物分送到指定的地點。

• Passage 2

Technical services and support are thought to be essential. Convention and exhibition centers are expected to provide technical services that are Increasingly sophisticate。Many clients will design audiovisual presentations and suggest the appropriate use of technology. At convention and exhibition centers, video projection of various kinds is available and is often used in conjunction with other media. Multimedia can Include video, computer-generated text and graphics, transfer of pictures from digital cameras and the insertion of sound or video into presentations. The other frequent technical issue is that of sound and the need for sound reinforcement, in all but the smallest events. To ensure that the required equipment is available, the venue management and technical staff should request that presenters come and test their material at least a week prior to the event.

Section 3 Speaking Activities

A. Specialized Terms

Match the expressions on the left with the best Chinese equivalent on the right.

1. booth number	A. 展台索引
2. closing date for applications	B. 人員雜費
3. one-stop services	C. 起租面積
4. Incidental expense	D. 英 / 中文楣板
5. service fee	E. 展台號
6. bank account number	F. 現場服務
7. minimum area	G. 服務費
8. on-site services	H. 英中文對照展覽指南
9. bilingual exhibition directory	I. 一條龍服務
10. English/Chinese stand fascia	J. 報名截止期

B. Sample Conversation

Listen and read aloud.

Situation: Mr. Li with the Dragon Translation Service is interviewing Ding Xiao for a job as an interpreter.

Woman:　Good afternoon, Mr. Li. I 've heard from Dragon Translation Service you want to hire an interpreter. I wonder if I could have the chance to get the position.

Man:　Good afternoon. .Please introduce yourself first.

Woman:　Yes, my name is Ding Xiao. I'm a native of Beijing and can speak standard Mandarin. Now I'm majoring in English in ECNU for nine years, and I also know a little French and GerMan.

Man:　You sound just the person we need. But sInce you are still a student, how can you do this job full-time?

Woman:　It is our summer holiday, and I'm free for almost two months.

Man:	That's fine. But have you interpreted at trade shows before and will you be able to interpret technical terms?
Woman:	Yes. I worked as an interpreter at last year's International Toy Exposition.
Man:	That's Good. When will you be available for the job?
Woman:	Any time. Our vacation has just started and I am free already..
Man:	Ok. Would you come to Hilton Hotel at 10 a.m. Thursday morning?
Woman:	Yes, of course. See you then,
Man:	That's really reasonable. Thank you very much for the information. I have to talk this with my teammates and let you know our decision in two weeks.
Woman:	I really appreciate that. If you have any question, please do not hesitate to contact me.
Man:	We will. Thanks again. Goodbye, Mr. Li.
Woman:	See you , Miss Ding.

C. Functional Expressions

Read aloud and practice with your partner.

1. What is on the list of renting?
2. Is the renting cost Included in the price for using the venue?
3. How much does it cost?
4. What is the price for renting one spotlight per day?
5. What should I do to hire an electrician?
6. Where should I settle the accounts?
7. Would you please the exhibition service desk?

D. Speaking Up

Render the following into English by using as many language skills learnt as possible.

1. 一張圓桌每天的租用費用是多少？
2. 充分的準備可以帶來完美的開始
3. 我們需要租些花卉和盆景，讓我們的展台更美觀。
4. 需要租什麼東西？
5. 請問請翻譯怎麼收費？

E. Role-play

Practice the conversations in English according to the situations.

• **Situation 1**

Mr. Smith is the representative of a textile company, which is planning to attend a textile show. He is asking for some information about the renting of facilities at the rental desk of the exhibition center. Mrs. Li is a clerk at the rental desk and she is answering Mr. Smith's questions and providing some suggestions.

• **Situation 2**

Two companies sponsored a volunteer effort to clean up the city's park. Two persons from the companies are discussing this event.

• **Situation 3**

Two staff members from an exhibiting company are discussing the rental of some equipments. Please try the Dialogue using your real names in pairs.

• **Situation 4**

Rose is working at the exhibition service desk. Now she is showing an exhibitor how to rent some necessary equipments and items.

Reference Answer

A. Specialized Terms

1.E 2.J 3.I 4.B 5.G 6.K 7.C 8.F 9.H 10.D

D. Speaking Up

1. How much do you charge for renting a round table per day?
2. Good preparation makes a perfect beginning.
3. What is on the list of renting?
4. We need to rent some flowers and plants to make our stand look much better?
5. How much does it cost to hire an interpreter?

Chapter 10
Safety and Security Service 安保服務

▌Section 1 Listening Activities

Go over the following words and expressions before listening to the tape.

amplification		n.	擴音器
infrared systems		n.	紅外系統
seating layout		a.	座位安排
overhead projector		n.	實物投影儀
shell schemes		n.	框架式展台
gangway		n.	過道
pendant mike		adv.	吊式話筒
roving mike			漫遊史話筒
adjustable			可調節的
keynote speakers			主旨發言人
cordless mikes			無線話筒
renovation			裝修
drapery			圍布
exterior			外飾
meticulously			謹慎地

A. Spot Dictation

A system of sound (1) _____ must be built into all large halls, with (2) _____ for changeover and sound balancing of each divided area if required. With large volume halls and high ceilings, line source speakers in (3) _____ are usually necessary.

(4) _____ may use hard-wired, induction loop or infrared systems. In most cases, the booths are purposely (5) _____ _____cubicles hired for the event, but suitable locations must be planned and (6) _____ provided.

(7) _____ may be permanently housed in a booth, back-stage area or adjacent room, or be temporarily set up within the hall when required. (8) _____

_____ As a guide, optimum viewing conditions for a flat screen are within 30 of the centerline and within a distance equal to two to six times the maximum screen width. (9) _____ _____, and higher if simultaneous camera views of the speaker are shown. (10) _____ _____

B. Multiple Choices

Directions: *In this section you will hear several Dialogues. After each Dialogue, there are some questions. Listen to the Dialogues carefully and choose the most appropriate answer to each question from the four choices marked A, B, C and D.*

• **Dialogue 1**

1. Where are the two speakers?

    In a restaurant.

    In a meeting room.

    At the airport.

    In a bank.

2. What might be the relationship between the two speakers?

    Host and hostess.

    Doctor and patient.

    Teacher and student.

    Meeting planner and organizer.

3. What are they talking about?

    They are talking about a projector.

    They are talking about a program.

    They are talking about a work.

    They are talking about a project.

4. What does Mr. Black mean?

    He means that the projector is old but pretty.

He means that the projector is old but pretty.

He means the projector is well maintained and works properly.

He means that the projector is old and pretty.

● **Dialogue 2**

5. Where are the two speakers?

   At a meeting.

   On a news-stand.

   At a venue.

   In a hospital.

6. What does the man think of the venue?

   It is the right site for his exhibits.

   It is beautiful.

   It seasonal.

   It is sweet.

7. What is the size of the woman's stands?

   They are 2m in width and 2.5m in height.

   They are 2m-3.5m in width and 2.5-3.0m in height.

   They are2.5-3.0m in width and 2m-3.5m in height.

   They are 2.5m in width and 2m in height.

8. We can infer from the talk that   .

   the man will design his own stand

   the man will bring in his own stand

   the man is not satisfied with the venue

   the man is satisfied with both the site and the stands

● **Dialogue 3**

9. What is the topic of the talk?

   Equipment.

   Meeting equipment.

   Microphone equipment.

Exhibition.

10. What kind of event is Mr. Smith inquire about?

A speech contest.

A lecture.

A conference.

An exhibition.

11. How many kinds of microphones are mentioned in the conversation?

Three.

Four.

Five.

Six.

12. What is the probable relationship between the two speakers?

Meeting manager and staff.

Meeting planner and organizer.

Meeting planner and sponsor.

Meeting sponsor and organizer.

C. Passage Dictation

Directions: *In this section, you will hear a passage. Listen carefully and write down what you hear on the tape.*

_____

_____

_____

_____

_____

_____

_____

_____

Tape script & Answers:

A. Spot Dictation

Tape script:

A system of sound (1) <u>amplification</u> must be built into all large halls, with (2) <u>facilities</u> for changeover and sound balancing of each divided area if required. With large volume halls and high ceilings, line source speakers in(3) <u>vertical columns</u> are usually necessary.

(4) <u>Simultaneous interpretation</u> may use hard-wired, induction loop or infrared systems. In most cases, the booths are purposely (5) <u>designed</u> and equipped cubicles hired for the event, but suitable locations must be planned and (6) <u>terminal</u> connections and access provided.

(7) <u>Projection equipment</u> may be permanently housed in a booth, back-stage area or adjacent room, or be temporarily set up within the hall when required. (8) <u>The location and size of the screen in relation to the seating layout is critical</u>. As a guide, optimum viewing conditions for a flat screen are within 30 of the centerline and within a distance equal to two to six times the maximum screen width. (9) <u>The bottom of the screen must be at least 1.8m above the platform</u>, and higher if simultaneous camera views of the speaker are shown. (10) <u>Facilities may be required for outside television and radio broadcasting services</u>.

B. Multiple Choices

Tape script:

• **Dialogue 1**

Mr.Blair   Mr. Black, is there any projector in this hall? It seems to me that you haven't one.

Mr.Black   No, we have, we really have one, Mr. Blair. There is it.

Mr. Blair   Oh, I see it. An overhead projector. But it looks old. Can it work properly?

Mr.Black   We have a dozen of engineers taking care of our equipment. And it did a pretty job at a meeting only a week ago.

● **Dialogue 2**

Man:	This environment is fitting in with our products. Then, what about your stands?
Woman:	For exhibits like yours, we usually provide shell schemes with divided booths or stands laid out in regular rows along gangways. Is it all right for you?
Man:	That's ok. How Many display stands have you got?
Woman:	Totally 10,000.
Man:	That's marvelous. What size do you have sInce I would like to make it sure they can match out products.
Woman:	Our modules are of international standard. They are 2m-3.5m wide and 2.5-3.0m deep. That gives an net area of 7.5m2-9.0m2.
Man:	Eh? I'm afraid they are not suitable for our products.
Woman:	It does not matter, sir. If necessary, we can extend them according to your requirement, or if you like, you can design your own.
Man:	Can we bring in our own stands?
Woman:	You are welcome to do that.

● **Dialogue 3**

Man:	Miss Johnson, can you tell me something about your microphones?
Woman:	Of cause, Mr. Smith. Actually, all of our business meeting halls, both large and small, are equipped with all kinds of microphones. They are at your service all the time.
Man:	You mean that we can have a pendant mike?
Woman:	That's for sure. And we also have a roving mike in every meeting room so that the speaker can roam freely around the stage or in audience.
Man:	Sounds nice. And what about your standing mikes. Are they adjustable?
Woman:	Absolutely. The standing mikes are attached to a mental stand from the floor, which, of course, can not be moved easily. But they can be adjusted to the height of the speaker.
Man:	How Many table mikes do you have in a meeting room of our size? You know we have invited several keynote speakers.
Woman:	We have three in each room. But if you need more, just note clearly how Many you need in the contract, and leave the rest to us.

Man: Eh... and the cordless ones. What if we need some cordless mikes? Well, you know they seem to be a little more convenient.

Woman: You said it. We have noticed that Many a meeting prefer cordless mikes sInce they are portable and need no electrical connection. We have four of this kind, ready to serve your meeting. Is it enough?

Man: Yes, I think so. Do you have a PA system, Mr. Johnson?

Woman: We surely have it, Mr. Smith. It is built in and is available for amplification in one or more rooms.

Man: That's fine. Thank you very much, Mr. Johnson. And I hope that I haven't caused too much trouble to you. You know I have to double-check before the meeting.

Woman: Oh, come on, Mr. Smith. I'm very glad to be at your service. And I hope our cooperation will be a great success.

Answers:

B 2. D 3. A 4. C 5. C 6. A 7. B 8. B 9. C 10. D 11. C 12. B

C. Passage Dictation

Tape script:

International Executive Housekeepers Association's 2005 Educational conference and convention in conjunction with ISSA-Interclean-USA'03 will be held October 14-17 2003, at McCormick place in Chicago Illinois. For housing purposes, IEHA has selected the Best Western Inn of Chicago located at 162 East Ohio Street. The inn has just recently undergone a dramatic renovation to ensure IEHA members the best possible nights of sleep.

While offering 350 tastefully decorated sleeping rooms that Include hair dryers, coffee makers, irons and ironing boards and Internet access, each guest room has all new furniture, carpeting, wallpaper, drapery and classic Chicago photograph. The inn of Chicago has also modernized the elevators, meticulously restored the exterior and renovated the spectacular open-aired 22nd floor Skyline Terrace. This hotel is extremely proud of its heritage and history, as well as its ability to adapt to the ever-changing needs of the client. Director of Housekeeping Peter Smith welcomes us to Chicago along with the entire staff of the inn.

Section 2 Interpretation Activities

A. Sentence Interpretation

1. First, find out the equivalents of the following words.

sanitation	
staff entrance area	
CCTV（closed circuit TV）cameras	
time-recording equipment	
保安代理機構	
有毒，易腐蝕或易燃性化學製品或氣體	
維護和保護	
遙控觀察和監控	

2. Read the following to your partner for him or her to put them down in Chinese or English.

1. Safety is a major consideration in all aspects of meeting, exhibition and hotel operation.
2. CCTV cameras fall into several categories.
3. Identification systems are commonly installed in the staff entrance area, together with time-recording equipment.
4. Theft by staff and service personnel is also a matter for concern.
5. Food and Beverage safety and sanitation is also essential to the success of a convention or exhibition.
6. 會議策劃者預定會議時應建議組織者負責危急情況的員警和保安代理機構。
7. 車輛出入口是需要安裝攝像機的關鍵地方。
8. 大樓內外區域的遙控觀察和監控是保安和管理經營中至關重要的部分。
9. 參展商應該負責自己參展品的維護和保護。我們建議照相機和其他貴重的小件物品應有人照看。
10. 未經科學展銷會安全官員同意的有毒，易腐蝕或易燃性化學製品或氣體，一律許展出。一般地應避免危險的化學製品。

B. Passage Interpretation

1. First, find out the equivalents of the following words.

burglar and fire alarm audio and video intercom 預防措施 人員受傷，財產損壞或者法律行為 嚴格執行	

2. Read the following passages to yourself and render them into Chinese or English.

● Passage 1

Supreme Security Systems is the largest independent, full-service electronic security provider in New Jersey. The company provides over 10,000 businesses, industrial facilities and residences with the most advanced burglar and fire alarms, closed circuit TV (CCTV) systems, access control systems and process and environmental monitoring systems, audio and video intercoms and music systems.

Your Answer

_____

_____

_____

_____

_____

_____

_____

_____

● Passage 2

把公共安全作為首要的必須考慮到的事情是至關重要的。應該採取適當的預防措施保證不會引起人員受傷，財產損壞或者法律行為等嚴重後果。所有展品都必須符合以下標準。安全人員也將嚴格執行這些標準。

Your Answer

_____

_____

_____

_____

_____

_____

_____

_____

_____

Reference Answer

A. Sentence Interpretation

1.

sanitation	衛生
staff entrance area	員工入口區
CCTV（closed circuit TV）cameras	閉路監控電視
time-recording equipment	考勤機
保安代理機構	security agencies
有毒，易腐蝕或易燃性化學製品或氣體	toxic, corrosive or flammable chemicals or gasses
維護和保護	maintenance and protection
遙控觀察和監控	remote observation and monitoring

2.

1. 安全是會議、展覽和飯店經營中各個方面都應考慮的主要事情。
2. 閉路電視攝像機有好幾種類型。
3. 身份識別系統一般都與考勤機一起安裝在員工入口處。
4. 員工和服務人員的偷竊也是要考慮的問題。
5. 食品飲料的安全與衛生也是會議或展覽成功的關鍵。
6. A meeting planner should advise the organizer of police and security agencies on risks at time of booking.
7. Vehicle entrances and exits are typical locations for cameras.

8. Remote observation and monitoring of areas inside and outside the building is an essential part of security and management operations.

9. Exhibitors are responsible for the maintenance and protection of their own exhibits during the Fair. We recommend that cameras and other expensive small items not be left unattended.

10. No toxic, corrosive or flammable chemicals or gasses are allowed unless approved by the Science Fair Safety Officer. In general, dangerous chemicals should be avoided.

B. Passage Interpretation

1.

burglar and fire alarm	盜竊和火災報警
audio and video intercom	視聽對講通訊裝置
預防措施	precautions
人員受傷，財產損壞或者法律行為	personal injury, property damage, or legal action
嚴格執行	be rigidly enforced

2.

● **Passage 1**

　　高級安全系統是新澤西洲最大的，獨立的 ' 和全面服務電子安全系統提供商。該公司為萬餘家商業，工業企業和居民客戶提供最高級的盜竊和火災報警，閉路電視系統，入口控制系統和過程與環境監控系統，視聽對講通訊裝置以及音樂系統。

● **Passage 2**

It is essential that safety to the public be a prime consideration. Suitable precautions must be taken to help ensure that serious consequences do not result in terms of personal injury, property damage, or legal action. All exhibits must conform to the following standards which will be rigidly enforced by the Safety Officer.

Section 3 Speaking Activities

A. Specialized Terms

Match the expressions on the left with the best Chinese equivalent on the right.

貴重物品	Fire prevention equipment
防火設備	Hidden property
威脅或危機評估	Valuables
隱蔽物品	Evacuation route
電腦犯罪 / 駭客	Hack
反入侵系統	Evaluation of threat and crisis
逃生路線	Monitor screen
監視屏	Identification PLATE
微波護欄	Statutory obligations
身份牌	Anti-invasion system
法律責任	Infrared guard

B. Sample Conversation

Listen and read aloud.

Situation: A meeting planner is checking the meeting safety and security measures with the organizer.

Planner: I'm told you've got a latest model of CCTV system. Then what kind of cameras do you use?

Organizer: Well, actually we are using several kinds of cameras, depending on the location, lens requirements and head operations.

Planner: Could you make it clear?

Organizer: Yes, Mr. Williams. We have cameras both indoor and outdoor with different angles of views.

Planner: What about lens?

Organizer: We have installed remote iris adjustment, footing and zooming ones. And for head operation, we have pans and tilt cameras.

Planner: And I think you also need to consider that positions of nearby lamps could shine into the lens and cause glare.

Organizer: You are right. We have solved this problem, and we also use silicon-vidicon cameras in parallel with infrared beams foe night vision.

C. Functional Expressions

Read aloud and practice with your partner.

What kind of cameras do you use?

Do you provide a lockable cupboard or storage area on the stand?

Can we have a name list of the security guards?

Be sure your valuable items are attended on your stand.

We offer 24 hour security service at the venue.

Flammable and explosive items should not be left unattended.

No toxic, corrosive or flammable chemicals or gasses are allowed unless approved by the safety officer.

Make it sure that heat sources must not be used near combustible materials.

Excuse me, Sir. We are the security officers of the venue. Can we have a look of your exhibits?

Excuse me, officer. One of our exhibits is missing. Can you help us to find it?

D. Speaking Up

Translate the following sentences into English by using as many language skills learnt as possible.

1. 請給我們一份保安人員的清單。
2. 我們提供 24 小時現場保安服務。
3. 易燃易爆物品須有專人保管。
4. 確保在易燃物品遠離熱源。
5. 我們是現場保安。請讓我們檢查一下您的展品。

E. Role-play

Practice the conversations in English according to the situations.

● Situation 1

Role A: You're an exhibitor who is planning to exhibit the latest products of your company at the 21ˢᵗ International Jewelry Exhibition that will be hosted by Shanghai New Century Exhibition Center. You are calling the center to consult the Security facilities to ensure your safety concerns about your exhibits. Your name is Peter Johnson.

Role B: You are a receptionist at Shanghai New Century Exhibition Center. Try to give Mr. Peter satisfactory answers to sooth his worries.

● Situation 2

Role A: You are the Meeting organizer of Grand Hotel. The annual meeting Canada Association of Stockers will be held in your hotel. Mr. David Hansen is now at your hotel to have an inspection. You are accompanying him. Answer his questions about safety and security concerns.

Role B: You are Mr. David Hansen, the meeting planner of Canada Association of Stockers. You are inspecting the meeting hotel so as to make sure about the security faculties to guarantee the success of the meeting. You concerns Include CCTV, the emergency exits and other details.

Reference Answer

A. Specialized Terms

1. C 2. A 3. F 4. B 5. E 6. J 7. D 8. G 9. D 10. H 11. I

D. Speaking Up

1. Can we have a name list of the security guards?
2. We offer 24 hour security service at the venue.
3. Flammable and explosive items should not be left unattended.
4. Make it sure that heat sources must not be used near combustible materials.
5. We are the security officers of the venue. Can we have a look of your exhibits?

Chapter 11
Helping with Post-Conference Logistics 會後物流服務

▌Section 1 Listening Activities

Go over the following words and expressions before listening to the tape.

mode of shipping		n.	運輸方式
delivery		a.	發貨 / 交貨
bulky		n.	大宗的
risk of theft		n.	盜險
ocean freight			海洋運輸
inventory			庫存 / 存貨
transit			轉運
the Bund			（上海）外灘
Yu Garden			（上海）愚園
CAAC（Civil Aviation Administration of China)			中國民航
airport shuttle bus			機場班車
CIP（cost' insurance and freight）price			到岸價
A.R.（all risks）			綜合險
F.P.A（free of particular average）			平安險
W.P.A（with particular average）			水漬險
B/L（bill of lading）			提單
the assured		v.	保險商
avert		n.	避免
carrier		n.	承運人
bailee		v.	受託人
claim		a.	索賠
defective		n.	受損的
container			集裝箱

A. Spot Dictation

The (1)_____ of Goods across borders and within countries can be accomplished through various (2)_____ of sea, air, and land (3)_____ used singly or in combination. In selecting the mode of (4)_____, we should

(5)_____ the product characteristics, destination,
(6)_____ of delivery and cost.

Large, bulky, low value-per-unit items and (7) _____ may not be economical to ship using certain forms of transportation, such as air freight. High-value items such as electronic components may have sufficient margins to allow for expensive rapid transportation, (8)_____.

Sometimes, the market may not be accessible by certain forms of transportation. For example, if Goods are shipped to Hong Kong from Guangzhong, ocean freight may be the first choice.(9)_____

_____. Rapid transportation enables the exporter to maintain fewer inventories in transit. The higher cost of transportation may well be more than offset by lower inventory carrying costs.(10)_____.

As noted above, however, this cost may be offset by reduced inventory carrying costs or justified by higher margin.

B. Multiple Choices

Directions: *In this section you will hear several dialogues. After each dialogue, there are some questions. Listen to the Dialogue carefully and choose the most appropriate answer to each question from the four choices marked A, B, C and D.*

• **Dialogue 1**

1. What can you learn from the dialogue?
   A. She will visit the Bund and Yu Garden.
   B. Because she has no interest in it. she won't do sightseeing after the exhibition
   C. Because she will visit her friend. she won't do sightseeing after the exhibition
   D. Because they are too crowded. she won't go to visit the Bund and Yu Garden

• **Dialogue 2**

2. When will the man leave for Beijing?
   A. On June 8.

B. On June 5.

C. On July 8.

D. On July 5.

● **Dialogue 3**

3. What do you think is the relationship between the two speakers?

    A. Clerk and exhibitor.

    B. Friends.

    C. Student and teacher.

    D. Passenger and driver.

4. When will the exhibitor arrive in Shanghai?

    A. Wednesday, April 25.

    B. Wednesday, June 24.

    C. Thursday, April 25.

    D. Thursday, June 24.

5. Where is the man's flight to?

    A. Pudong international Airport, Shanghai.

    B. Hongqiao International Airport, Shanghai.

    C. Beijing Capital International Airport.

    D. Hong Kong International Airport.

6. What can you infer from the dialogue?

    A. Mr. Clinton won't arrive on time.

    B. Mr. Clinton may take the airport shuttle bus.

    C. Mr. Clinton will choose to take a taxi to get to the center.

    D. The clerk is not helpful.

7. Where is Mr. Clinton now?

    A. At Hongqiao International Airport.

    B. At the Convention and Exhibition Center.

    C. In New York.

    D. Not mentioned.

• Dialogue 4

8. What are they talking about?

   A. Shipment.

   B. Insurance.

   C. Invoice.

   D. B/L.

9. What do you know about F.P.A?

   A. It is Good for delicate Good.

   B. It is enough for Goods that are not easy to break.

   C. All consignors would like to get F.P.A.

   D. Mr. Harriet won't get F.P.A.

10. What does W.P.A cover?

   A. It covers all risks.

   B. It covers the same amount as F.P.A does.

   C. It doesn't cover any loss of particular average.

   D. It covers the loss of particular average.

11. What is not mentioned in the dialogue?

   A. Insurance rate.

   B. A.R.

   C. F.P.A.

   D. W.P.A.

12. What statement is not true?

   A. Mr. Harriet would get F.P.A for his Goods.

   B. Mr. Harriet came for the information in the morning.

   C. Mr. Harriet would like to get insurance for tires.

   D. The clerk is very helpful.

C. Passage Dictation

Directions: *In this section, you will hear a passage. Listen carefully and write down what you hear on the tape.*

_____

_____

_____

_____

_____

_____

_____

_____

_____

Tape script & Answers

A. Spot Dictation

Tape script:

The (1) <u>movement</u> of Goods across borders and within countries can be accomplished through various (2) <u>forms</u> of sea, air, and land (3) <u>transportation</u> used singly or in combination. In selecting the mode of (4) <u>shipping</u>, we should (5) <u>take into consideration</u> the product characteristics, destination, (6) <u>required speed</u> of delivery and cost.

Large, bulky, low value-per-unit items and (7) <u>basic commodities</u> may not be economical to ship using certain forms of transportation, such as air freight. High-value items such as electronic components may have sufficient margins to allow for expensive rapid transportation, (8) <u>which also offers less risk of theft</u>.

Sometimes, the market may not be accessible by certain forms of transportation. For example, if Goods are shipped to Hong Kong from Guangzhong, ocean freight may be the first choice.

(9) <u>Speed is a significant factor for some products because of its effect on inventory</u>. Rapid transportation enables the exporter to maintain fewer inventories in transit. The higher cost of transportation may well be more than offset by lower inventory carrying costs.

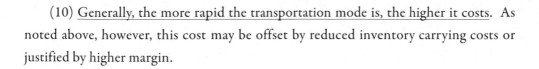

(10) <u>Generally, the more rapid the transportation mode is, the higher it costs.</u> As noted above, however, this cost may be offset by reduced inventory carrying costs or justified by higher margin.

B. Multiple Choices

Tape script:

● **Dialogue 1**

Man:	I hear the Bund and Yu Garden is the most visited places.
Woman:	Yes, no visitor to Shanghai wants to miss the chance of visiting them.
Man:	Shall we do some sightseeing after the exhibition?
Woman:	I'd love to, but I have promised to visit one of my American friends working in Shanghai?
Man:	What a pity!

● **Dialogue 2**

Man:	Good morning, Madam. May I help you?
Woman:	Yes. I want to reserve two round flight tickets to Beijing. I'm going to attend a conference there after the exhibition?
Man:	Ok. What airline do you want to fly and when are you leaving?
Woman:	Any flight on CAAC. I plan to leave on June 5, and return on June 8.
Man:	Lucky you are. There are still some tickets available.
Woman:	When shall I get the tickets?
Man:	You can get the E-tickets right away.

● **Dialogue 3**

Woman:	Hope Convention and Exhibition Center. May I help you?
Man:	Yes, I'm John Clinton calling from New York. We are planning for the exhibition trip to hope Convention and Exhibition Center. Would you give me some advice?
Woman:	My pleasure. I'll be glad if I could be of any help. What can I do for you?
Man:	We're leaving for Shanghai tomorrow and arriving on Wednesday, April 25. You know I'm a complete stranger to Shanghai. I really don't know how to get to your center?

Woman:	Which airline will you fly?
Man:	Airline China.
Woman:	Is your flight to Pudong International Airport, or to Hongqiao International Airport?
Man:	It is to Hongqiao International Airport.
Woman:	We have an airport shuttle bus, which takes our guests back to the center every thirty minutes.
Man:	That's great. Thank you for the info.
Woman:	Always at your service.

● Dialogue 4

Woman:	Good morning, sir. How can I help you?
Man:	Yes. I'm Michael Harriet. I'd like to ask you a few questions about insurance?
Woman:	I hope I could be of any help.
Man:	We're given a CIP price for some toys. What insurance do you suggest I would get?
Woman:	SInce toys are not easy to break, you won't want A.R.. F.P.A is enough.
Man:	I don't know what A.R. and F.P.A cover.
Woman:	A.R. covers all risks while F.P.A covers the safe delivery of the commodity.
Man:	What about the partial loss of the nature of particular average?
Woman:	F.P.A doesn't cover it but W.P.A does.
Man:	Therefore, F.P.A will do. By the way, could you arrange it for me?
Woman:	No problem. We can make it.
Man:	What documents should I submit?
Woman:	Be sure to bring the Invoice No. or B/L No.
Man:	Thank you very much for your help.
Woman:	You are welcome.

Answers

1. C 2. B 3. A 4. A 5. B 6. B 7. C 8. B 9. B 10. D 11. A 12. C

C. Passage Dictation

Tape script:

It is the duty of the Assured and their Agents, in all cases, to take such measures as may be reasonable for the purpose of averting or minimizing a lose and to ensure that all rights against Carriers, Bailees or other third parties are properly preserved and exercised. In particular, the Assured or their Agents are required.

To claim immediately on the Carriers, Port Authorities or other Bailees for any missing packages.

In no circumstances, except under written protest, to give clean receipts where Goods are in doubtful condition.

When delivery is made by Container, to ensure that the Container and its seals are examined immediately by their responsible official. If the Container is delivered damaged or with seals broken or missing or with seals other than as stated in the shipping documents, to clause the delivery receipt accordingly and retain all defective or irregular seals for subsequent identification.

Section 2 Interpretation Activities

A. Sentence Interpretation

1. First, find out the equivalents of the following words.

1. innovation		7. 經裝修一新	
2. attendance		8. 音像設備	
3. distraction		9. 省去 …… 的麻煩	
4. keynoter		10. 滿足要求	
5. attendee		11. 會議套餐	
6. limo （limousin）			

2. Read the following to your partner for him or her to put them down in Chinese or English.

1. Where you want to go will determine what method to get there. For example, if you want to go downtown, you may have a few options, like bicycle, taxi, limo, or bus.

2. If a reservation is needed, first you need to check availability.

3. Delivery of the ticket is usually quick: it is even faster to book an e-ticket.

4. Business class passengers may also choose the maglev to the airport, where they will board their airplane.

5. Drop off, pickup, and transfers can all cause problems if the language or transportation systems are very different than those the passenger has at their home.

6. 一般來說，有三種主要的交通方式，即地面交通、軌道和航空。

7. 國際多式聯運（multimodal transport）是指兩國間根據多式聯運合約，採用至少兩種運輸方式，將貨物從發貨地運往目的地。

8. 出口貨物常常採用集裝箱運輸。集裝箱運輸對多式聯運尤其適合。

9. 在交通方面，有很多問題發生在下客、搭載和轉乘時。

10. 全程運輸中當貨物不轉運，直接從裝貨港運至目的港，承運人或其代理就簽發給托運人（shipper）一張直運提單。

B. Passage Interpretation

1. First, find out the equivalents of the following words.

methods of delivery		東西高架	
cargo space		南北高架	
mark		輕軌	
waybill			
consignment			
dispatch			

2. Read the following passages to yourself and render them into Chinese or English.

● Passage 1

　　Normally, the bill of lading contains detailed provisions about the methods of delivery and the cessation of the carrier's liability. Regardless of the kind of carrier to be used, the carrier will issue a "booking contract", reserving space for the cargo on a specified vessel. We shall be glad to know the time of transit and frequency of sailing, and whether cargo space must be reserved; if so, please send us the necessary application forms. The Goods have been packed and marked exactly as directed so that they may be shipped as soon as possible. A waybill, giving full particulars, will be sent to you as soon as the consignment is ready for dispatch by Eastern Airlines.

Your Answer

_____

_____

_____

_____

_____

_____

_____

_____

● **Passage 2**

　　上海還存在另一個與北京和洛杉磯類似的大問題，那便是上海太大了，上海的計程車司機通常會說他們只熟悉浦東或浦西。交通主幹道包括東西高架、南北高架，地鐵一號線、二號線和輕軌明珠線。

Your Answer

_____

_____

_____

_____

_____

_____

_____

_____

Reference Answer

A. Sentence Interpretation

1.

1. innovation	創新	7. 經裝修一新	completely renovated
2. attendance	參加會議的人數	8. 音像設備	audiovisual equipment
3. distraction	干擾物	9. 省去 ...... 的麻煩	save the trouble
4. keynoter	主旨發言人	10. 滿足要求	meet one's demand
5. attendee	與會者	11. 會議套餐	meeting package
6. limo (limousin)	豪華轎車，旅遊客車，豪華中巴		

2.

1. 你的目的地將決定你選擇什麼樣的交通工具。比方說，如果你要想去市中心，你可能有好幾種選擇，如自行車、計程車、豪華中巴和公共汽車。

2. 如果需要預訂，你首先要查票務資訊，確認是否有票。

3. 送票通常很快，如果預定的是電子票，速度更快。

4. 公務艙的乘客也可能選擇乘磁懸浮去機場乘飛機。

5. 如果乘客語言不通且又完全不熟悉當地交通系統，那麼他們在下客、搭載和轉乘時都可能碰到麻煩。

6. In general, there are three main kinds of transportation, ground, rail and air.

7. International multimodal transport means the conveyance of cargo between two countries by at least two models of transport from the place of dispatch to that of destination on the basis of a multimodal transport contract.

8. The transportation of export Goods is frequently carried out in containers, which are particularly suitable for multimodal transport.

9. One difficult part where a lot of problems happen in transportation is in drop, pickup and transfers.

10. Direct bill of lading is issued by the carrier or his agent to the shipper when the Goods are transported directly from the port of loading to that of destination without transshipment during the whole voyage.

B. Passage Interpretation

1.

methods of delivery	遞交方式	東西高架	East-west Elevated Highway
cargo space	貨艙	南北高架	South-north Elevated Highway
mark	嘜頭	輕軌	Light rail
waybill	運貨單		
consignment	委託		
dispatch	派發，派譴		

2.

● **Passage 1**

通常，提單包含交貨方式、承運人責任截止期等資訊。不論採取何種運輸方式，承運人都需要簽訂一份「訂艙合約」，預訂好指定貨船上的艙位。請告知運輸時間有多長、有多少航次、貨艙是否需要預定。如需要預訂，請將訂艙表寄來。貨物已嚴格按照要求包裝妥當，刷好嘜頭，以便儘快運出。貨物備妥，東方航空公司發運時，我們會把一份載明明細的空運單寄給你們。

● **Passage 2**

Shanghai has one more major problem in common with Beijing and Los Angeles. It is so big! Taxi drivers often will say they know Pudong well, or Puxi well. Major transportation networks Include the east-west elevated highway the north-south elevated highway, Metro Line 1, Line 2 and the Light Rail Line 3.

Section 3 Speaking Activities

A. Specialized Terms

Match the expressions on the left with the best Chinese equivalent on the right.

1. shipping specialist   _____ A. 運費表

2. forwarding agent   _____ B. 郵資

3. destination   _____ C. 專業輸送

4. postage   _____ D. 損失

5. tariff   _____ E. 目的地

6. damage   _____ F. 總帳單

7. price catalogue   _____ G. 價格表

8. freight rate   _____ H. 運輸代理

9. dispatch   _____ I. 發送

10. master account   _____ J. 運輸費

B. Sample Conversation

Listen and read aloud.

Situation: Mr. Hilton, meeting planner, is in a hurry on his way to the convention service manager's office. He is wondering if the convention service manager (CSM) could help find him a express delivery company to handle the bulky meeting stuff.

CSM： Good morning Mr. Hilton. Is there anything I can do for you?

Hilton: I'm looking for a delivery company. You know, the conference has come to a successful close. And there stuffs to be sent back home. Can you suggest a company to take care of them?

CSM： Yes. We have in-house delivery service right here. We are shipping specialists and can provide you excellent service.

Hilton: Oh, that'll be wonderful. We really appreciate your service in the past. And I have trust in your staff.

CSM： Thank you, Mr. Hilton. May I ask what kind of materials you'd like to deliver?

Hilton: We have name signs of the attendees that we want to reuse at next conference, some meeting documents, and some other stuff.

CSM： That's quite a lot. But don't worry. Our crew can handle them professionally and promptly. We are faster than airlines. Where do you want them?

Hilton: To San Francisco. Here is our address.

CSM： I see. Then how quickly do you need them delivered?

Hilton: Is it possible that our headquarters will receive them in two days?

CSM： It depends. If the packages are ready by now, it will take less time for our employees to move. Have you packed them in advance?

Hilton: No, we haven't. I wonder if you could help.

CSM： No problem. We also have professional packing crew and adequate packing facilities. But it will Incur extra charge for the packing.

Hilton: You may charge it and the freight rates to our master account. What are the rates for the packing and the delivery service?

CSM： Here's the price tag, sir. Please take a look at it. As you can see, our prices are quite competitive in the city.

Hilton: Well, sure reasonable. I need a guarantee that the package will be there.

CSM： We do guarantee if you agree to the terms of delivery.

Hilton: Ok. I don't see there is any problem.

CSM： Now please sign your name on the contract here, and here, the names of the objects to be delivered. We'll send our people up to handle the packing right away.

C. Functional Expressions

Read aloud and practice with your partner.

Common questions for convention express delivery or shipment

What kind of material you'd like to deliver?

Where do you want them?

How soon do you want them to reach the destination?

How quickly do you need them delivered?

Do you agree with the payment terms?

May I suggest express delivery be made?

Would you please take a look at the tariff?

Could you make a list of further instructions about shipment of convention materials?

May I know when we could expect the delivery?

Do you guarantee that the packet will be there on time?

Could you deliver the packet immediately?

Can't you make the delivery a little earlier?

What's the earliest possible date then?

What are the rates of the packeting and the delivery service?

D. Speaking Up

Understand the speaker's intention, and then fill in the blanks.

1. ⸺ _____.

——The earliest time of delivery is 4 days form now.

（用意：詢問收貨日期）

2. ——_____?

——No problem. We can deliver the packet in an hour to meet your requirement.

（用意：要求儘快起運）

3. ——_____?

——This kind of packeting costs more.

（用意：詢問包裝費用）

4. ——We want these materials to reach our destination by Christmas？

—— _____.

（用意：建議快遞服務）

5. ——_____?

——We enforce the packets with iron straps.

（用意：詢問包裝方式）

E. Role-play

Practice the conversation in English.

A：希爾頓先生，你能確定所有被租用的設備都列在物品清單上了嗎？

B：讓我看看，兩台錄音設備，一台投影儀，三個麥克風。是的，全齊了。

A：會議一結束，供應商就會馬上把設備運走嗎？

B：我恐怕到時他們不會馬上來。你能安全保管這些物品並把他們交還給供應商嗎？

A：當然可以，我們會把這些設備保護好的。

B：那些標識牌則麼辦？下次會議我們還要用的

A：這個我們也想到了。我們的服務員會收集所有的標識牌，然後交還給你們。

B：那太好了，我真的很感謝你們的細心幫助。運輸費用怎麼算？

A：220 元人民幣。

B：好的，把費用記在總帳單上。

A：我們會照辦的。

Refernece Answer

A. Specialized Terms

1. C　2. H　3. E　4. B　5. A　6. D　7. G　8. J　9. I　10. F

D. Speaking Up

1. When can the delivery be made?
2. Can you make the deliver as soon as possible?
3. What do you charge for the packeting?
4. We would suggest the express delivery service.
5. How do you packet these boxes?

Chapter 12
Opening and Reception 開幕與酒會

▌Section 1 Listening Activities

Go over the following words and expressions before listening to the tape.

boost	v.	推進，提高
visibility	n.	能見度
infrastructure	n.	基礎結構，基礎設施
the International Bureau of Exposition(IBE)		國際博覽局
refreshment	n.	點心
sales representative	a.	銷售代表
R&D (research and development)	v.	研發
call filter		電話過濾
thriving		繁榮的
highlight		突出，強調

A. Spot Dictation

The great (1)_____ held in London in 1851 was (2) _____ the first (3) show to be called (4) _____. SInce then there have been 31 (5)_____ and many cities have (6) _____ _____ have a world fair. In 1928 (7) _____ _____ was founded in Paris to co-ordinate these events and ensure that there is only one each year. (8) _____ _____ _____. The stated objectives Include encouraging trade, Increasing the visibility of a city and country, developing tourism, attracting economic development and Increasing employment, (9) _____ _____, the celebration of a past event, and the entertainment of the masses, as well as the often unstated one of obtaining extra funds from the higher level of government. (10) _____

_____ , but as well as selling the city, there is also the selling of ideas.

B. Multiple Choices

Directions: *In this section you will hear several dialogues. After each dialogue, there are some questions. Listen to the dialogue carefully and choose the most appropriate answer to each question from the four choices marked A, B, C and D.*

● **Dialogue 1**

1 What is the woman doing?

    A. She is visiting the exhibition.

    B. She is looking for his booth.

    C. She is asking the way.

    D. She is looking for someone in his company.

2. What is the booth number?

    A. 28-A.

    B. 28-B.

    C. 27-A.

    D. 27-B.

● **Dialogue 2**

3. Where does this conversation take place?

    A. At home.

    B. In Mr. Lin's company.

    C. In a hotel.

    D. In an exhibition.

4. What is Mr. Lin asking about?

    A. His room.

    B. His mail.

    C. His booth.

    D. His car.

• Dialogue 3

5. What are the two speakers mainly talking about?

   A. A magazine about electronics.

   B. A company called "James".

   C. An exhibition in Chicago.

   D. A high-tech printer.

6. Who is James Lin?

   A. He is a sales manager.

   B. He is a sales representative.

   C. He is an engineer.

   D. He is an editor of the magazine.

7. How many countries will be attending the exhibition in Chicago?

   A. About 100.

   B. About 80.

   C. About 60.

   D. About 40.

8. Where is the Woofers Inc. based?

   A. In shanghai.

   B. In Taiwan.

   C. In Chicago.

   D. In New York.

• Dialogue 4

9. What is the product mentioned in the Dialogue?

   A. A kind of computer.

   B. A kind of catalog.

   C. A kind of phone.

   D. A kind of business card.

10. What can the product do?

   A. It can save the company a lot of money by cutting down wasted telephone time.

   B. It can have up to one hundred extensions.

   C. It has a type of call filter.

D. It can do all of the above.

11. When will this product be on the market?

    A. At the beginning of next month.

    B. Tomorrow.

    C. Next year.

    D. Not mentioned.

12. What can the customers do if they have any questions?

    A. Read the catalog.

    B. Give the salesperson a call.

    C. Go to the factory.

    D. Go to the market.

C. Passage Dictation

Directions: *In this section, you will hear a passage. Listen carefully and write down what you hear on the tape.*

_____

_____

_____

_____

_____

_____

_____

_____

Tape script & Answers

A. Spot Dictation

Tape Script:

The great (1) <u>exhibition</u> held in London in 1851 was (2) <u>probably</u> the first (3) <u>show</u> to be called (4) <u>a world fair</u>. SInce then there have been 31 (5) <u>universal exhibitions</u> and many cities have (6) <u>sought to</u> have a world fair. In 1928 (7) <u>the International Bureau of Exposition</u> was founded in Paris to co-ordinate these events and ensure that there is only one each year. (8) <u>There are various and interlinked objectives for holding a world fair</u>. The stated objectives Include encouraging trade, Increasing the visibility of a city and country, developing tourism, attracting economic development and Increasing employment, (9) <u>stimulating the re-use of land and infrastructure improvements</u>, the celebration of a past event, and the entertainment of the masses, as well as the often unstated one of obtaining extra funds from the higher level of government. (10) <u>The prime motive for holding a world fair is to boost the city</u>, but as well as selling the city, there is also the selling of ideas.

B. Multiple Choices

Tape Scripts:

• Dialogue 1

Woman: Excuse me, sir! Could you tell me where the service desk is located?

Man: Sure. It's right over there, to the right of our refreshment stand.

Woman: Hello! I'm Susan Lin from Woofers Inc. Do you know where I can find my booth?

Man: You're in booth number 28-A. Here's a map of the exhibition hall, and here we are at the service desk.

Woman: OK, and where exactly is our booth? ... Oh! There it is. Thanks for your help.

• Dialogue 2

Woman: Good evening, sir. Welcome to Royal Fantasis Hotel. How can I help you?

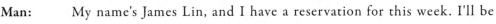

Man: My name's James Lin, and I have a reservation for this week. I'll be attending the electronics exhibition beginning tomorrow.

Woman: Of course, Mr. Lin, we've been expecting you. You'll be staying in Room 611. Would you please sign the register? ... Here.

Man: Certainly. By the way, do you know if there is any mail for me? I'm expecting some from overseas.

Woman: Nothing has arrived yet, but we'll let you know as soon as we get anything.

● Dialogue 3

Man: Excuse me, I notice you're reading an electronics magazine. Did you know there's a big electronics exhibition in Chicago starting tomorrow?

Woman: Of course! That's why I'm going to Chicago. Hi! My name's Linda Miller. What's your name?

Man: James Lin. I'm a sales representative for Woofers Inc., based in China. Are you looking forward to the exhibition?

Woman: I've been waiting to go to this show for more than three months. There are going to be companies from over forty different countries.

Man: I know. I'm really looking forward to seeing what products will be on market next year.

Woman: I'm more interested in the new discoveries which are being made in the electronics industry.

Man: Really? Do you mind if I ask what part of the electronics industry you're in?

Woman: Not at all. I work in the R&D department of a company based in Los Angeles. We specialize in producing printers.

Man: What's the name of your company? Maybe I've heard of it.

Woman: I don't think so. We're just a little company called "Halcyon"

Man: Hmm. Oh, didn't you come out with an amazingly small but strong high-tech printer at the exhibition last year in New York?

Woman: Yeah, that turned out to be our best seller of the year, but everyone forgets our name.

● Dialogue 4

Woman: Good morning, sir. I see you're looking at the "Dinger". It's the latest model of computerized phone.

Man:	It looks very impressive, but so do a lot of the products here. What can it do?
Woman:	The "Dinger" can save your company a lot of money by cutting down on wasted telephone time.
Man:	That sounds Good, but could you tell me about each function in detail?
Woman:	Here, take a catalog. This will show you why the "Dinger" is the best value for your money.
Man:	Excuse me. Could you tell me about the call filter function on this model? I think this function can save a lot of time.
Woman:	Right. Only the "Dinger" has this type of call filter. When there's an incoming call, the number will appear on the digital display screen.
Man:	So, if you know the number of the person who is calling, you can then decide if you want to answer the phone.
Woman:	Exactly. Why don't you take this catalog, my card is attached. If you have any questions after the exhibition closes, just give me a call.
Man:	How Many extensions can this phone have?
Woman:	It can have up to one hundred extensions. It is very convenient for a large or busy office.
Man:	Thanks. When will this product be on the market?
Woman:	All of the products you see here will be on the market at the beginning of next month. Do you have a business card?
Man:	Yes, of course. Here it is. If you give me a call tomorrow, after I have a chance to read the catalog, we can get together and talk.

Answers:

1. b 2. a 3. c 4. b 5. c 6. b 7. d 8. b 9. c 10. d 11. a 12. b

C. Passage Dictation

Tape script:

The Shakespeare Festival Australia began as a 12-day festival in April 1997, celebrating the works of William Shakespeare. It is presented by the Southern Highlands Institute for the Performing Arts, a non-profit, Incorporated association formed to build a performing arts center in the southern highlands district of New South Wales. This area has declining rural and manufacturing sectors, shrinking blue-collar industries and Increasing youth unemployment. A thriving tourism industry will assist the area's economy.

The festival was developed with two goals: firstly, as a new arts event to highlight the need for a performance and educational center and, secondly, to attract visitors to the region during autumn. We decided to hold the first festival to coIncide with Shakespeare's birthday on 23 April.

Section 2 Interpretation Activities

A. Sentence Interpretation

1. First, find out the equivalents of the following words.

1. booth		8. 畫架	
2. function book entries		9. 分時預訂	
3. entrée		10. 交錯預訂	
4. specialty or theme restaurant		11. 點菜單	
5. appetizer		12. 單獨定價	
6. spicy		13. 套餐，公司餐	
7. tart		14. 固定價格	

2. Read the following to your partner for him or her to put them down in Chinese or English.

1. The current trend toward light cuisine is continued at most banquet luncheons. Fish and chicken are the entrées of choice with many meeting planners. Formal luncheons offering heavy sauces, rich desserts, and alcoholic beverages spell trouble to most planners and have therefore declined in popularity.

2. Easels, chart boards, movie screens, tables for projectors, and extension cords are Included in function room rental rates while computers for PowerPoint presentations, VCRs, slide projectors, overhead projectors are charged separately.

3. The use of reservation is a convenience and service to guests as well as a tool that helps staff members recognize guests by name, guarantee speed and quality of service, and promote production efficiency.

4. There are two basic types of reservation systems—interval reservations and staggered reservations. The interval reservations system offers seating at specific intervals during the meal period while the staggered reservations system staggers seating during the entire meal period and reservations can be made for any time that tables are available during the meal period.

5. An a la carte menu is a menu which offers choices in each course and in which each item is individually priced and charged for. A table d'hote menu offers some (usually limited) choices and is charged at a fixed price for the whole menu.

6. 預訂員填寫訂單時應該獲取以下資訊：以誰的名義預訂，名字的正確寫法，預訂的時間和日期，人數，需要有煙還是無煙區，一般餐桌還是包廂，有無特殊要求，以及客人的電話號碼。

7. 餐飲任務登記一般包括團名、客戶姓名、頭銜和電話號碼；預計出席人數；項目名稱以及活動類型。

8. 對於多數會議型飯店來說，宴會的收入僅次於客房。

9. 主菜通常最先點。主菜包括牛肉、豬肉、魚和沙拉（涼拌菜）等。許多特色餐館或主題餐館提供的主菜種類相對較少，這樣可以最大程度地減少內部烹調和服務問題。

10. 開胃菜包括水果汁或番茄汁、乳酪、水果和海鮮類。開胃菜是就餐前用來開胃的，因此他們的量一般較小，通常帶辛辣味或酸味，咬上去口感好。

B. Passage Interpretation

1. First, find out the equivalents of the following words.

1. specialty menu		9. 生的 / 地	
2. cereal		10. 半成品的	
3.waffle		11. 領班	
4. watchword		12. 助理	
5. take-out		13. 跑菜員	
6. pasta dish		14. 副領班	
7. lasagna		15. 服務站	
8. linguine		16. 廚師	

2. Read the following passages to yourself and render them into Chinese or English.

● Passage 1

Cart Service is called "French Service" in the United States and in Germany; yet in France, Cart Service is referred to as "Russian Service". The food is brought to the guests' table in either a raw state or a semi-prepared state and finished in front of the guests in the dining room on a cart. The final food preparation is performed by the chef de rang, and he/she is assisted by a commis de rang. Although the chef de rang has been called a captain or a waiter, he/she performs some of the tasks performed by a waiter and some of the tasks a captain usually performs. The commis de rang is referred to as a bus boy but performs many more service-related functions than is usually given a bus boy. A demichef de rang is a commis de rang who has recently been promoted and is given a small station as well as the assistance of a commis.

The chef de rang and the commis work together as a team in a station of approximately twenty guests. The chef de rang prepares the food and places the food on the plates, while the commis actually serves the guest. Each of these two individuals must be highly skilled, sInce the chef de rang is performing many of the functions in the dining room that the cook performs in the kitchen.

Your Answer

_____

_____

_____

_____

_____

_____

_____

_____

● Passage 2

功能表的定價方式有三種，他們是套餐價、零點價以及零點和套餐相結合的定價方式。套餐功能表給整餐提供一個價格。零點菜單上，每道菜、每種飲料都列出來單獨定價。

　　三種基本的菜單為早餐、午餐和晚餐。特色功能表是為了吸引特定的客戶群體或滿足特定的市場需求。

　　典型的早餐功能表提供水果、果汁、蛋類、穀物、薄煎餅、華夫餅以及像熏肉、香腸一類供早餐用的肉食。早餐功能表上的品種要遵循簡單、快捷和價廉的原則。

　　午餐客人通常比較匆忙，午餐功能表以三明治、湯和沙拉為主，這些菜製作起來相對簡單快捷。午餐功能表上的菜通常比晚餐清淡，不如晚餐那麼精緻。

　　對於大多數人來說晚餐是一天中的正餐。典型的晚餐主菜有牛排、烤肉、雞肉、海鮮以及像鹵汁麵條和寬麵條一類的義大利麵點。葡萄酒、雞尾酒和外地風味甜點更有可能出現在晚餐功能表上而不是午餐功能表上。

　　一般的特色功能表包括兒童餐單、老人功能表、含酒精類飲料功能表、甜點功能表、房內用膳功能表、外賣功能表、宴會功能表和民族特色功能表。

Your Answer

_____

_____

_____

_____

_____

_____

_____

Reference Answers

A. Sentence Interpretation

1.

1. booth	包廂	8. 畫架	easel
2. function book entries	餐飲任務登記	9. 分時預訂	interval reservations
3. entrée	主菜	10. 交錯預訂	staggered reservations
4. specialty or theme restaurant	特色或主題餐館	11. 點菜單	a la carte menu
5. appetizer	開胃菜	12. 單獨定價	be individually priced

| 6. spicy | 辛辣的 | 13. 套餐，公司餐 | table d'hote menu |
| 7. tart | 酸的 | 14. 固定價格 | fixed price |

2.

1. 目前多數午餐宴請趨向於選用清淡的飲食。許多會議策劃者選擇魚和雞肉作為主食。正式的午餐提供難以消化的調味汁、甜得發膩的甜點和酒精飲料，這種午餐給多數會議策劃者招惹麻煩，已經越來越不受歡迎。

2. 功能廳（宴會廳）的租賃價格中包括畫架、告示板、幕布、投影台和接線，而PPT 演示用的電腦以及錄影機、幻燈機、投影儀則需單獨付費。

3. 預訂一方面給客人提供方便，另一方面可以使員工知道客人的姓名、保證服務的速度和品質，提高烹調效率。

4. 基本的餐飲預訂系統有兩種——分時預訂和交錯預訂。分時預訂給客人提供特定的用餐時間，而交錯預訂則指給客人交錯安排座位，只要在整個用餐時間有空桌就可預訂。

5. 零點功能表是指可以選擇每道菜並且每道菜單獨定價和收費的菜單。套餐功能表則提供較為有限的幾種選擇，而且整個功能表通常有固定的定價。

6. Reservation-takers should obtain the following information from callers: the correct spelling of the name the reservation will be under, the date and time of the reservation, the number in the party, whether a smoking or non-smoking section is preferred, whether the guests want a table or a booth, special instructions, and the guest's phone number.

7. Function book entries typically Include the group's name; the client's name, title, and phone number; the estimated attendance; the name of the event; and the type of event.

8. For most convention hotels, banquet functions are second only to the sale of guestrooms in generating revenue.

9. Entrées are usually selected first. They Include beef, pork, fish, entrée salad, etc. Many specialty or theme restaurants offer relatively few entrées. This minimizes many in-house production and serving problems.

10. Appetizers Include fruit or tomato juice, cheese, fruit, and seafood items. Appetizers are supposed to enliven the appetite before dinner, so they are generally small in size and spicy or pleasantly biting or tart.

B. Passage Interpretation

1. First, find out the equivalents of the following words.

1. specialty menu	特色菜單	9. 生的 / 地	in a raw state
2. cereal	穀物	10. 半成品的	semi-prepared
3.waffle	華夫餅	11. 領班	chef de rang
4. watchword	口號，格言	12. 助理	commis de rang
5. take-out	外賣	13. 跑菜員	bus boy
6. pasta dish	義大利麵點	14. 副領班	demichef de rang
7. lasagna	闊麵條，鹵汁麵條	15. 服務站	station
8. linguine	扁麵條	16. 廚師	cook

2.

●Passage 1

在美國和德國，餐車服務被叫作法式服務；但是在法國，這種服務指的是俄式服務。食物在生的或者是半成品狀態下拿到客人的桌上，並且在餐廳的餐車上當著客人的面製作成成品。成品食物由領班準備，一般會有一個助理協助他。雖然領班一直被稱作組長或服務員，他 / 她既要承擔服務員的工作又要做領班的工作。助理指跑菜員，但他要比一般的跑菜員履行更多與服務相關的職責。副領班是新近被提拔的助理，他負責一個小型服務站，並有助理來協助他。

領班和助理組成一組，他們的服務站大約有 20 個客人。領班準備食物、給食物裝盤，真正給客人上菜的是助理。領班要在餐廳裡完成廚師在廚房完成的許多工作，這樣，他們每個人就必須有精湛的手藝。

●Passage 2

The three types of menu pricing styles are table d'hote, a la carte, and combination table d'hote/ a la carte. A table d'hote menu offers a complete meal for one price. With an a la carte menu, food and beverage items are listed and priced separately.

Three basic types of menus are breakfast, lunch, and dinner menus. Specialty menus appeal to a specific guest group or meet a specific marketing need.

Breakfast menus typically offer fruits, juices, eggs, cereals, pancakes, waffles, and breakfast meats like bacon and sausage. The watchwords for breakfast menu items are "simple", "fast", and "inexpensive".

SInce lunch guests are usually in a hurry, lunch menus must feature menu items that are relatively easy and quick to make, such as sandwiches, soups, and salads. Lunch menu items are usually lighter and less elaborate than dinner menu items.

Dinner is the main meal of the day for most people. Steaks, roasts, chicken, seafood, and pasta dishes like lasagna and linguine are typical dinner entrées. Wines, cocktails, and exotic desserts are more likely to be on a dinner menu than on a lunch menu.

Common specialty menus Include children's, senior citizens', alcoholic beverage, dessert, room service, take-out, banquet, and ethnic.

Section 3 Speaking Activities

A. Specialized Terms

Match the expressions on the left with the best Chinese equivalent on the right.

1.	a la carte	A.	開瓶費
2.	cash bar	B.	餐飲零點
3.	continental breakfast	C.	單獨付費酒吧
4.	corkage	D.	法式服務
5.	covers/ head count	E.	大陸式早餐
6.	French service	F.	客人人數
7.	guarantee	G.	最多人數
8.	luncheon	H.	主題晚會
9.	plated buffet	I.	裝盤式自助餐
10.	refreshment break	J.	包餐，公司餐
11.	table d'hote	K.	早中飯
12.	theme party	L.	茶點時間

B. Sample Conversation

Listen and read aloud.

Situation 1: A reservationist is receiving a telephone call from the president of "Green Cities", who wants to book a banquet for Friday.

Booking a Reception

Staff: Good morning. New International Conference and Exhibition Center. How may I help you?

Customer: Good morning. This is Brown, President of "Green Cities". I'd like to reserve a banquet for Friday.

Staff: What time would you like it?

Customer: At 7:00.

Staff: How Many in your party?

Customer: 80.

Staff: Well, our Lotus Hall will do.

Customer: Could we take up the menu choice now?

Staff: Sure.

Customer: As for the menu choice, we'd like the routine entrée and chef's choice for the banquet.

Staff: How would you like the banquet to be served?

Customer: French service. By the way, can you preset the furniture for the banquet before 6:30 p.m.?

Staff: Sure. We will take care of it.

Customer: What is the minimum you charge for each attendee?

Staff: RMB300 per person, premium brands excluded.

Customer: How are call brands charged?

Staff: Usually by the bottle, but we can also charge by the drink.

Customer: I prefer the latter. Is there any service charge for it?

Staff: Yes. There will also be other charges, such as corkage if drinks are brought from outside.

Customer: Well, in this case, house brands would be fine.

Staff: OK, Mr. Brown.

Customer: May I put the charges on to the master account?

Staff: Yes. Anything else I can do for you?

Customer: That's all.

Sample Closing and Thank-you Speech

Listen and read aloud.

Situation 2: Mr. Brown is President of the symposium, which is coming to a close. He is now holding a dinner party for the attendees and making a closing and thank-you speech.

> Mr. Vice President,
> Our American friends,
> My colleagues,
> Ladies and gentlemen,
> On behalf of all the members of mission, I would like to express our sIncere thanks to you for inviting us to such a marvelous dinner party.
> We really enjoyed the delicious food and excellent wine. Also, the music was perfect. I enjoyed meeting and talking to you, and sharing the time together. As we say, well begin is half done. I hope we will be able to maintain this Good relationship and make next year another great one.
> Thank you again for the wonderful part, we had a great time.
> In closing, I would like to invite you to join me in a toast.
> To the health of Mr. Vice President.
> To the health of our American friends.
> To the health of my colleagues.
> And to all the ladies and gentlemen present here.
> Cheers!

C. Functional Expressions

Read aloud and practice with your partner.

Receiving a reservation call
Good morning. Chinese Restaurant. Reservations. How may I help you?
Good afternoon. Western Restaurant. What can I do for you?

Time
When would you like your table, sir?
How many people are there in your party, sir?
Could you please tell me the number of diners, sir?

Guest's name and telephone
May I have your name and telephone number, sir?
Could you please tell me your name and telephone number, sir?

Your name and telephone number, please?

Under whose name, please?

Requirements

Any other requirements?

Anything special, please?

Confirmation

So, it's Mr. White, a table for five at 6:30 p.m. this evening. Am I right?

A table near the window for Mr. White for 3 at 12:00. Am I right?

A table for 3 this evening under the name of Mr. White. Will that be all right?

How to summarize a conference

We have come to the end of the...

I wish I could give you a meaningful summary of...

It is quite impossible for me to summarize the proceedings, but I would like to mention...

How to express thanks

I would like to thank...

I wish to thank...

On behalf of..., I wish to express our sIncere gratitude to...

Thank you again for...

How to announce the next conference or congress

It is a privilege for me to announce that the next...to be held in...

I now have the duty and the honor to declare the...officially closed.

Now I declare the conference closed.

How to propose a toast

In closing, I would like to invite you to join me in a toast.

Let's drink a toast to...

Let me propose a toast to the health of...

To..., cheers!

D. Speaking Up

Render the following into English by using as many language skills learnt as possible.

1. 大會已近尾聲，組委會的全體成員由衷感謝所有與會者的通力合作。

2. 雖然我難以把大會上的每一件事情都加以總結，但是我想把一些檔中的重點提一下。

3. 感謝主席、發言者以及所有與會者所作的貢獻。

4. 我代表組委會的所有成員，向你們表示真誠的感謝，是你們使這次研討會如此成功。

5. 現在，我榮幸地宣佈大會正式閉幕。

6. 在結束之際，我想邀請各位一起舉杯祝酒。為在場的所有女士們、先生們，乾杯！

E. Role-play

Render the following into English by using as many language skills learnt as possible

● **Situation 1**

A headwaiter is receiving a telephone call from a local customer to book a none-smoking table for a party of six for tonight.

● **Situation 2**

You are the emcee of a conference. Please extend an address on the closing ceremony. Cover the following points when delivering the speech.

1. Summarizing the congress briefly

2. Expressing thanks to all the participants for their contributions

3. Announcing the next congress will be held in 2007

4. Announcing the conference closed

● **Situation 3**

You are the president for a seminar. Now you are holding a farewell party. Please extend a closing speech and propose a toast. Cover the following points when delivering the speech.

1. Summarizing the four-day seminar, which has greatly benefited all the participants

2. Best wishes to all the participants

3. Proposing a toast

Reference Answer

A. Specialized Terms

1-b   2-   c   3-e   4-a   5-f   6-d   7-g   8-k   9 - i

10-l   11-j   12-h

D. Speaking Up

1. We have come to the end of the Congress. The members of our Organizing Committee are deeply grateful for the hearty cooperation of all participants.

2. It is quite impossible for me to summarize the proceedings, but I would like to mention some of the prIncipal points that have emerged from some of the papers.

3. I wish to thank all the chairmen, speakers and other participants for their valuable contributions.

4. On behalf of all the members of our organizing committee, I wish to express our sIncere gratitude to all of you who have made the seminar such a success.

5. I now have the honor to declare the congress officially closed.

6. In closing, I would like to invite you to join me in a toast. To all the ladies and gentlemen present here, cheers!

Chapter13
Attending the Event 參加展會

▌Section 1 Listening Activities

Go over the following words and expressions before listening to the tape.

BRT (bus rapid transit)		n.	專用公交系統
congestion		v.	交通阻塞
optimize		v.	優化
integrate		n.	整合
commuter			通勤者，每日往返上班者
port of discharge		ad.	卸貨港
airport representative		n.	機場代表
promptly			立即
liability			責任

A. Spot Dictation

The city will set up a series of rapid bus lines over the next five years to improve its public (1)_____system, according to the Shanghai Urban Transport Management Bureau.

Building BRT lines is an (2)_____and economical approach for Shanghai to help enhance its mass (3)_____efficiency and ease (4)_____. By 2010, the city is expected to have (5)_____of Bus Rapid Transit lines, Including 30 to 50 kilometers of BRT lines in (6)_____and 70 to 100 kilometers in (7)_____.
The BRT lines will be set up (8)_____
_____. They will become a Good supplement to the metro system. (9)_____
_____.

Shanghai's current metro network doesn't cover enough of the city to meet commuter demand.(10)_____
_____

B. Multiple Choices

Directions: *In this section you will hear several Dialogues. After each Dialogue, there are some questions. Listen to the Dialogues carefully and choose the most appropriate answer to each question from the four choices marked A, B, C and D.*

● **Dialogue 1**

1. Why can't Hongyuan be chosen as the port of discharge?
    A. Because it is not convenient to discharge Goods there.
    B. Because there is no port of discharge.
    C. Because he doesn't choose to discharge Goods there.
    D. Because the clerk docsn't agree to discharge Goods there.

● **Dialogue 2**

2. What does Mr. Johnson ask the clerk to do for him?
    A. To claim the exhibits.
    B. To take care of him.
    C. To send him the B/L.
    D. To reserve a booth.

● **Dialogue 3**

3. What are they talking about?
    A. Delivering the exhibits on display.
    B. Description of the Goods.
    C. Shipping-related companies.
    D. Airlines.

4. When will the exhibition close?
    A. On Tuesday.
    B. On Thursday.
    C. In two days.
    D. Tomorrow.

5. How does Mr. Daniel deal with the exhibits?

A. He wants them to be consigned back by air.

B. He wants them to be consigned back by sea.

C. He wants them to be mailed back.

D. He wants them to remain where they are.

6. Why does Mr. Daniel decide on delivery by sea?

A. It is fast.

B. It is cheaper.

C. It is not far.

D. It is convenient.

7. What statement is not true?

A. Mr. Daniel is an exhibitor.

B. His exhibits are very huge.

C. He would like to consign the exhibits by sea?

D. The Clerk is not very helpful.

● Dialogue 4

8. When will Toy 2005 be held?

A. May 20.

B. May 26.

C. May 15.

D. May 5.

9. What does Mr. Howard want to do?

A. He wants to reserve a booth.

B. He wants to visit the convention and exhibition center.

C. He wants to visit Miami.

D. He wants to reserve a ticket.

10. How can Mr. Howard make the reservation?

A. By EMS.

B. By phone.

C. By mail.

D. On line.

11. How often does the airport shuttle bus take guests to the center?

A. Every two hours.

B. Once an hour.

C. Every half hour.

D. Three times a day.

12. What statement is true?

A. Mr. Howard is calling to book a flight ticket.

B. Hope Convention and Exhibition Center may send Mr. Howard an E-mail confirming his reservation.

C. Mr. Howard will have to make a face-to-face reservation.

D. Mr. Howard is calling to cancel his reservation.

C. Passage Dictation

Directions: *In this section, you will hear a passage. Listen carefully and write down what you hear on the tape.*

_____

_____

_____

_____

_____

_____

_____

_____

_____

_____

_____

_____

_____

_____

_____

_____

_____

_____

Tape script & Answers:

A. Spot Dictation

Tape script:

The city will set up a series of rapid bus lines over the next five years to improve its public (1)transport system, according to the Shanghai Urban Transport Management Bureau.

Building BRT lines is an (2) effective and economical approach for Shanghai to help enhance its mass (3) transit efficiency and ease (4) congestion. By 2010, the city is expected to have (5) 100 to 150 kilometers of Bus Rapid Transit lines, Including 30 to 50 kilometers of BRT lines in (6) downtown areas and 70 to 100 kilometers in(7) the suburbs. The BRT lines will be set up (8) like a subway system, with stations along set routes. They will become a Good supplement to the metro system. (9) The lines are expected to handle 20 percent of the city's commuters every day after they are completed.

Shanghai's current metro network doesn't cover enough of the city to meet commuter demand. (10) Shanghai hopes that the BRT lines will help to integrate and optimize the city's bus line network.

B. Multiple Choices

• Dialogue 1

Woman:	Good morning, sir. What can I do for you?
Man:	I'm Wang Dong. I'd like to ask you some questions about shipping order.
Woman:	My pleasure. Go ahead, please.

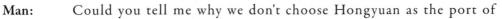

Man:	Could you tell me why we don't choose Hongyuan as the port of discharge?
Woman:	There is no port of discharge there.
Man:	I see. Thank you for the info.
Woman:	You are welcome.

• Dialogue 2

Woman:	Convention and Exhibitor Center. Anything I can do for you?
Man:	Yes. I'm Jack Johnson calling California. I have shipped our exhibits to Shanghai. Could you arrange for me to claim them?
Woman:	We can make it for you. Please send us your B/L.
Man:	OK. I'll take care of it right away. Thank you.
Woman:	I'm always at your service.

• Dialogue 3

Woman:	Good afternoon, sir. What can I do for you?
Man:	Good afternoon. Yes. I'm Daniel. Could you make it for us to ship the exhibits on display?
Woman:	Yes, we could.
Man:	You know the exhibition is coming to a close in two days. They're very huge and I want to consign them back.
Woman:	We could arrange for the related company. How would you like to ship your exhibits, by air or by sea?
Man:	By sea. I don't want them to be shipped by flight this time. It is very expensive.
Woman:	We could make it for you to book containers for delivery.
Man:	How long will it take me to get the exhibits?
Woman:	We shall give 40 days.
Man:	Fine.
Woman:	Would you please fill in this registration form?
Man:	OK. (After a while...) Is that all right?
Woman:	Yes. We'll take care of it.
Man:	Thank you for your help.
Woman:	You're welcome.

• **Dialogue 4**

Woman: Hope Convention and Exhibition Center. May I help you?

Man: Yes. I'm John Howard calling from Miami. I'd like to reserve a booth for Toy 2005 on May 5.

Woman: You may log on our Website to make an online reservation.

Man: Smart move.

Woma Be sure to give us your E-mail address so that we can inform you once your reservation is confirmed.

Man: By the way, could you tell me how to get to your center?

Woman: You may either take a plane or come by sea?

Man: I prefer to fly there. It's fast and comfortable. Do you have the airport shuttle bus?

Woman: Yes, it leaves by the hour.

Man: How can I find it?

Woman: No worry. You can contact our airport representative desk there. They will help you.

Man: That's fine. Thank you for the info. Goodbye.

Woman: Thank you for calling, Mr. Howard. We are looking forward to your coming. Goodbye.

Answers:

1. b 2. a 3. a 4. c 5. b 6. b 7. d 8. d 9. a 10. d 11. b 12. b

C. Passage Dictation

Tape script:

The Consignees or their Agents are recommended to make themselves familiar with the Regulations of the Port Authorities at the port of discharge.

To enable claims to be dealt with promptly, the Assured or their Agents are advised to submit all available supporting documents without delay, Including when applicable:

1. Original policies of insurance.

2. Original or certified copy of shipping invoices, together with shipping specification and/or weight notes.

3. Original or certified copy of Bill of Lading and/or other contract of carriage.

4. Survey report or other documentary evidence to show the extent of the loss or damage.

5. Landing account and weight notes at port of discharge and final destination.

Correspondence exchanged with the Carriers and other Parties regarding their liability for the loss or damage.

Section 2 Interpretation Activities

A. Sentence Interpretation

1. First, find out the equivalents of the following words.

門市價 前提條件	
well-established	
trade visitors	

2. Read the following to your partner for him or her to put them down in Chinese or English.

1. 展會組織者的服務物件有兩個：一個是參展商，一個是參觀者，他們參加展會的目的各不相同。

2. 現在有越來越多的展會由會展專業人士組織，但是出於經濟原因還是有很多的展會是由機構自行組織的。

3. 大多數的資深人士傾向于認為在什麼樣的場所舉辦展會比在什麼地區舉辦更重要。

4. 酒店的標準價稱作門市價，但是商務客人很少按門市價付款。

5. 餐飲設施與服務是商務旅遊活動取得成功的必要的前提條件。

6. In many countries, where there is an accommodation classification system, there may seem to be little relationship between quality and the official grade.

7. Organizers should ensure that they allow a margin of error so that if delays occur the event schedule will not be disrupted.

8. The informal networking is often the most part of the event, and organizers should plan opportunities for it to take place.

9. The well-established event attracts large numbers of trade and public visitors because it uses a highly professional venue with excellent facilities for both exhibitors and visitors.

10. The organizer should have a clear idea of what the ideal venue would be for their event, together with a checklist of criteria to test any venue against.

B. Passage Interpretation

1. First, find out the equivalents of the following words.

refunds space assignment Cancellations lease terminated defaulted rebate written authorization	
官方指定承運商 參展指南 安裝與拆卸 承諾遵守 進場與出場 消防規定 非易燃品	

2. Read the following passages to yourself and render them into Chinese or English.

● Passage 1

Payments and refunds: The balance of the space rental charge is due and payable on or before Nov. 1, 2009. Applications received without payments will not be processed nor will space assignment be made. Cancellations received before Nov.1, 2009 will receive a refund of money paid, less 20% of the value of the original booth order. All requests for refund must be received in writing. NO REFUNDS WILL BE MADE AFTER Nov.1, 2009.

Show management: If The Exhibition is not held for any reason, the rental and lease of space to the exhibitor shall be terminated. In such case, the exhibitor will get the full refund of the amount of already-paid-for spaces.

The organizer has the right to use space without payment by Nov. 1 to suit its own convenience, Including selling the space to another exhibitor, without any rebate or allowance to the defaulted exhibitor. Each exhibitor must apply for his own space and no exhibitor will be permitted to assign any part of his space to another firm without written authorization from show management.

Your Answer

_____

_____

_____

_____

_____

_____

_____

_____

_____

● **Passage 2**

運輸須知

運輸必須有官方指定承運商裝運。承運商位址可參看《參展指南》。

展品的安裝與拆卸：所有展品必須在 2009 年 11 月 21 日展會開幕兩小時前安裝完畢。在 2009 年 11 月 23 日展會結束前，不得拆卸展品。參展商承諾遵守展會管理者關於進場與出場的規定。

消防規定：每個展位所展示的物品必須是非易燃品。參展商必須承諾遵守所有消防規定。

參展商服務指南：關於展位色彩選擇，展位空間設計，展攤設施等資訊，參展商應該詳細閱讀《參展商服務指南》。《參展商服務指南》一般于展會舉辦前 60 天發至參展商手中，或者在展位費用付清後獲得。

Your Answer

_____

_____

_____

_____

_____

_____

_____

_____

Reference Answers

A .Sentence Interpretation

1. First, find out the equivalents of the following words.

2.

1. An exhibition organizer usually has two audiences, namely exhibitors and visitors, each with different desires.

2. There is clearly a trend towards the use of professional organizers but many organizations still prefer in-house organizations largely for financial reasons.

3. Most respected commentators appear to suggest that the specific building or buildings where the event will take place should take precedence over the geographical location.

4. Standard prices in hotels are called the rack rate but very few business clients will pay this price.

5. Food and beverage is an essential prerequisite for successful business tourism events.

6. 許多國家都有酒店等級分類標準，但是這些等級分類常常與品質好壞沒什麼關係。

7. 組織者務必要留有餘地，萬一遲延，也不會影響整個展會的排程。

8. 非正式的交流是展會的主要活動，組織者應該為此提供方便。

9. 這個著名的展覽會吸引了大量的業內人士和一般公眾，展會的場所非常專業化，設施精良，能夠同時滿足參展商和參觀者的需要。

10. 組織者對展會舉辦的要求要十分明確，對每一個舉辦地按照詳細的標準來進行評價。

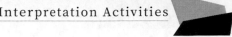

B. Passage Interpretation

1.

refunds	退款
space assignment	展位分配
Cancellations	取消預訂
lease	租約，租期
terminated	終止
defaulted	未履約
rebate	補償
written authorization	書面同意
官方指定承運商	official drayage contractor
參展指南	Exhibitor Manual
安裝與拆卸	Exhibit installation and dismantling
承諾遵守	agree to abide by
進場與出場	move-in/move-out
消防規定	Fire regulations
非易燃品	flame retardant

2.

● **Passage 1**

　　付款與退款

　　展位租借費請於 2009 年 11 月 1 日前付清。未按時付款的申請不予受理，不予租借展位。2009 年 11 月 1 日前取消預訂，已付款者可獲得原展位費 80% 的退款。所有退款申請須以書面形式遞交。2009 年 11 月 1 日後不予退款。

　　展會管理

　　如果展會不能舉行，展位租借合約終止。參展商將獲得已付展位租借費的全額退款。

　　組織者對 11 月 1 日前未付費的展位享有自由處置權，包括可以將展位賣於別家參展商，未履約參展商不得進行抗辯或提出補償請求。參展商必須自己申請展位，不得未經展會管理者書面同意而私自將展位任一部份劃作其他參展商使用。

● **Passage 2**

　　Shipping instructions: Shipments should be sent to the official drayage contractor. The address will be provided in the Exhibitor Manual.

Exhibit installation and dismantling: All exhibits must be completed and in place two hours prior to the opening of the exposition at on Nov.21, 2009. No exhibitor may commence the dismantling of his exhibit until the show closes on Nov. 23, 2009. Exhibitors agree to comply with the move-in/move-out schedule provided by show management.

Fire regulations: All materials used as display items in individual booths must be flame retardant. Exhibitors must agree to abide by all applicable rules and regulations of the City Fire Code.

Exhibitor's information and service manual: To develop your booth color scheme, layout, furniture requirements, etc., exhibitors should read the Exhibitor's Service MANUAL. This information will be in your hands 60 days prior to the exposition, or after payment for space has been made.

Section 3 Speaking Activities

A. Specialized Terms

Match the expressions on the left with the best Chinese equivalent on the right.

● Part 1

1. non-stop flight	A. 不定期客票
2. CAAC	B. 會議接龍
3. charter flight	C. 定期客票
4. back to back	D. 停車場服務員
5. taxi dispatcher	e. 揚招計程車
6. open ticket	f. 中途不停站的直達航班
7. OK ticket	g. 中國民航
8. parking attendant	h. 包機飛行
9. limousine	i. 計程車調度
10. to hail a taxicab	j. (機場、車站) 接送旅客的交通車

● Part 2

1. first class	A. 二等艙

2. business class	B. 商務級艙位
3. economy class	C. 國家航空公司
4. upgrade	D. 固定乘客
5. round trip	e. 登機證
6. charter flight	f. 艙壁座
7. coach	g. 頭等艙
8. boarding pass	h. 普通座位
9. frequent flyer	i. 往返旅行
10. flag carrier	j. 提高級別
11. bulk head	k. 水上運輸公司
12. freight forwarder	l. 包機飛行

B. Sample Conversation

Listen and read aloud.

Situation: An exhibitor telephones the Event Manager to ask him to book flight tickets for her.

Manager: Can I help the next person in line please?

Exhibitor: I'd like to get a flight to Beijing on April 18th and return on the 21st.

Manager: May I know your name and room number, please?

Exhibitor: Louis Fortell, Room 1108.

Manager: How Many traveling in your party, sir?

Exhibitor: Just one.

Manager: There are several flights to Beijing. When would you like to leave?

Exhibitor: Let's see. I'd like to catch an early flight out and return in the evening on the 21st.

Manager: All right. A flight leaves Shanghai at 6:00 A.m. arriving in Beijing at 8:45. Is that too early?

Exhibitor: No, that's fine. And what about the return?

Manager: An 8:00 p.m. flight arrives back in Shanghai at 10:45 p.m. How does that sound to you?

Exhibitor: Sounds Good.

Manager: Okay, I'll check that for you with the airport booking office.

Exhibitor: When can I get the tickets?

Manager: Please come again at 4:00 p.m. this afternoon, and we'll let you know if the tickets are available.

Exhibitor: Okay, thanks for your help.

C. Functional Expressions

Read aloud and practice with your partner.

Getting ticket booking information

How many traveling in your party, sir?

What airline would you prefer?

When would you like to leave?

How about the return?

Giving flight information

A flight leaves Shanghai at 6:00 A.m. arriving in Beijing at 8:45. Is that too early?

An 8:00 p.m. flight arrives back in Shanghai at 10:45 p.m. How does that sound to you?

Giving ticket information

I'll check that for you with the airport booking office.

Please come again at 4:00 p.m. this afternoon, and we'll let you know if the tickets are available.

D. Speaking Up

　　Render the following into Chinese by using as many language skills learnt as possible.

A： 國際旅行社。有何吩咐？

B： 我想瞭解從上海飛往紐約的航班資訊。

A： 請問你的出行時間有什麼安排？

B： 至少在一月七日前到達紐約，12 日返回上海。

A： 我知道。我們有去紐約的直達航班。320 航班在一月六號上午八點從上海起飛，當天下午兩點到達紐約。

B: 那麼回程票呢？

A: 回程是一月十二號上午八點從紐約起飛的 334 航班，第二天上午十點到達上海。

B: 需要飛行多長時間。

A: 十八小時二十分種。

B: 天哪，要這麼長時間。請問票價多少？

A: 往返票價一共 8,900 人民幣元。

B: 好的。請幫我預訂這兩趟航班。

A: International Desk. How may I help you?

B: Yes, I'd like to check on flights from Shanghai to Yew York.

A: When are you planning on traveling?

B: I need to be in New York by January 7th at the latest and return on the 12th.

A: I see. We have a direct flight to New York. You could leave Shanghai on Flight 320 at 8:00 a.m. on January 6th, arriving in New York at 2:00 p.m. the same day.

B: And what about the return?

A: You'd leave Yew York on Flight 334 at 8:00 a.m. on January 12th, arriving in Shanghai at 10:00 a.m. the following day.

B: How long is the trip?

A: Eighteen hours and twenty minutes.

B: Oh, my! That's a long flight! And how much is it?

A: The round-trip ticket is 8,900 yuan RMB.

  B: OK, I think I'd like to go ahead and make a reservation.

E. Rolc-play

Practise the following in English by using as many language skills learnt as

You are at the travel agent, giving and receiving the following information concerning flight reservation. Make a dialogue with your partner, you being the first to open the conversation.

Destination:	
Departure date:	
Number in party:	
Special request:	
Flight:	
Return flight:	

Price of he round-trip ticket:	
Length of the flight:	

Reference Answer:

A. Specialized Terms

● **Part 1**

1. f 2. g 3. h 4. b 5. i 6. a 7. c 8. d 9. j 10. e

● **Part 2**

1. g 2. b 3. h 4. j 5. i 6. l 7. a 8. e 9. d 10. c 11. f 12. k

D. Speaking Up

A: International Desk. How may I help you?

B: Yes, I'd like to check on flights from Shanghai to Yew York.

A: When are you planning on traveling?

B: I need to be in New York by January 7th at the latest and return on the 12th.

A: I see. We have a direct flight to New York. You could leave Shanghai on Flight 320 at 8:00 a.m. on January 6th, arriving in New York at 2:00 p.m. the same day.

B: And what about the return?

A: You'd leave Yew York on Flight 334 at 8:00 a.m. on January 12th, arriving in Shanghai at 10:00 a.m. the following day.

B: How long is the trip?

A: Eighteen hours and twenty minutes.

B: Oh, my! That's a long flight! And how much is it?

A: The round-trip ticket is 8,900 yuan RMB.

B: OK, I think I'd like to go ahead and make a reservation.

Chapter 14
Reserving Post Conference Tours 會後旅遊預訂

▊ Section 1 Listening Activities

A. Spot Dictation

Go over the following words and expressions before listening to the tape.

encompass		v.	步道
trails		n.	熱帶的
tropical		a.	遺產
heritage		n.	
Window of the World		a.	世界之窗
all-in-one package			一攬子計畫，包價
gala night			盛大晚會
Bay Crossing Bridge			跨海大橋
compulsory			必要的
insurance policy			保險單
insurance premium			保險費
excursion		n.	遠足旅遊
forward		v.	運送，轉交

These are optional ticketed (1) _____ tours.

Art Lover's Tour Take 2. You'll love the Andy Warhol Museum, the most comprehensive single-artist museum in the world. This unique museum, (2) _____, encompasses an extensive collection of work by the pop art prInce and Pittsburgh native. After the tour, stay on the North Side and enjoy a meal at the (3) _____.

A Trip to The Strip. The Strip District is a Pittsburgh (4) _____ _____ street vendors, fresh fish, produce, cheeses and ethnic markets from every nationality. Eat your way around the world in this (5) ____ _____ at Kaya, an award-winning local restaurant that features Island cuisine and festive tropical drinks.

Pittsburgh Cycling Tour. Pittsburgh's three rivers are lined with (6) _____ _____. You'll ride at a moderate pace along several miles of one of Pittsburgh's many flat riverfront trails. Along the way, (7) _____.

Cultural District Walking Tour. Once a former "red-light" district, the Cultural District today is one of the best places for the arts in the country. You'll (8) _____ _____ _____. Afterwards, hear live jazz outdoors, and then cap off the day with cocktails and light fare at The Backstage Bar.

B. Multiple Choices

• **Dialogue 1**

1. Which of the following sights is not Included in the package tour?
   A.   The Alps Indoor Ski Dome.
   B.   Pyramid Fantasy Hall.
   C.   The Eiffel Tower.
   D.   Amazon Forest and Fuji Digital Cinema.

2. How much do the tickets cost?
   A.   Two yuan for each.
   B.   Fifty yuan for two.
   C.   One hundred yuan in all.
   D.   Fifteen yuan for each.

• **Dialogue 2**

3. Whom does the man intend to call?
   A. Any travel agent at Contourist.
   B. The travel agent at Contourist he called last week.
   C. Manager of Contourist.
   D. None of the above.

4. Why does the man call the travel agency?

A. To make a booking for a post-con tour in Shanghai for his group.

B. To make a booking for a tour in Shanghai for his wife and him.

C. To make a booking for a post-con tour in Ningpo for his group.

D. To make a booking for a tour in Ningpo for his wife and him.

5. How many people will be in the party?

A. 2.

B. 3.

C. 12.

D. 20.

6. What is the man's telephone number at work?

A. 0171 321 5454—22.

B. 0181 328 5252—22.

C. 0181 328 5215—22.

D. 0171 321 1554—22.

7. On which date will the tour start?

A. 30th of June.

B. 13th of June.

C. 30th of July.

D. 13th of July.

8. What is the insurance premium?

A. Ten pounds per head.

B. One pound per head.

C. Seventeen pounds per head.

D. Twenty pounds per head.

9. How much should Mr. Morgan pay as a deposit?

A. 80 pounds.

B. 1600 pounds.

C. 360 pounds.

D. 16 pounds.

10. When will Mr. Morgan pay the deposit?

A. Immediately after the telephone conversation is over.

B. The beginning of next week.

C. The end of this week.

D. Not given.

C. Passage Dictation

Directions: *In this section, you will hear a passage. Listen carefully and write down what you hear on the tape.*

_____

_____

_____

_____

_____

_____

_____

_____

_____

_____

Tape script & Answers:

A. Spot Dictation

Tape script:

These are optional ticketed (1) <u>post event</u> tours.

Art Lover's Tour Take 2. You'll love the Andy Warhol Museum, the most comprehensive single-artist museum in the world. This unique museum, (2) <u>housed in a former factory</u>, encompasses an extensive collection of work by the pop art prInce and Pittsburgh native. After the tour, stay on the North Side and enjoy a meal at the (3) <u>locally owned restaurant</u>.

A Trip to The Strip. The Strip District is a Pittsburgh (4) <u>landmark neighborhood where you'll find</u> street vendors, fresh fish, produce, cheeses and ethnic markets from every nationality. Eat your way around the world in this (5) <u>guided two-hour walking tour, followed by tasty dinner</u> at Kaya, an award-winning local restaurant that features Island cuisine and festive tropical drinks.

Pittsburgh Cycling Tour. Pittsburgh's three rivers are lined with (6) <u>wonderful bike trails full scenic beauty</u>. You'll ride at a moderate pace along several miles of one of Pittsburgh's many flat riverfront trails. Along the way, (7) <u>you'll cross over some of Pittsburgh's famous bridges, and learn about the region's heritage</u>.

Cultural District Walking Tour. Once a former "red-light" district, the Cultural District today is one of the best places for the arts in the country. You'll (8) <u>visit six world-class performing arts venues, more than a dozen art galleries, and enjoy public art projects and award-winning parks along the way</u>. Afterwards, hear live jazz outdoors, and then cap off the day with cocktails and light fare at The Backstage Bar.

B. Multiple Choices

● Dialogue 1

At the Ticketing

Staff; Welcome to Window of the World. May I help you, sir?

Visitor: I'd like two admission tickets, please.

Staff; OK. We offer the all-in-one package.

Visitor: What does the package Include?

Staff; You pay once for all the six tours and services.

Visitor: What do I expect to see at these places?

Staff; You may enjoy various forms of entertainment at the World Square. Besides, the Alps Indoor Ski Dome, Grand Canyon Flume Ride, Pyramid Fantasy Hall, Amazon Forest and Fuji Digital Cinema enable you to enjoy the endless fun brought by technologies.

Visitor: Sounds fantastic. What about other sights? Do I need to pay extra for them?

Staff; Yes, I'm afraid so. But if you stay at 7:30 p.m. you may enjoy the songs and dances at the gala night free of charge.

Visitor:	I see. Can you give me a program schedule and a map?
Staff;	Here you are. They are free.
Visitor:	How much is each ticket?
Staff：	RMB 50 Yuan for each. Did you say you need two?
Visitor:	Yes, here is the money.
Staff;	Thank you, sir. Here are the tickets. By the way, may I recommend to you our restaurants at the International Street?
Visitor:	Can I have food in European style?
Staff;	Certainly, sir.
Visitor:	Very Good. Thanks. Goodbye.
Staff;	Take you time. Have a nice day, sir.

Question 1: Which of the following sights is not Included in the package tour?

Question 2: How much do the tickets cost?

● **Dialogue 2**

Travel Agent:	Good morning, Contourist. How can I help you?
Conference Planner:	Hello, er...yes. Can I speak to Celine?
Travel Agent:	Er, yes. Who's calling?
Conference Planner:	I spoke to her last week about a post-con travel in Shanghai and I'd like to make a booking.
Travel Agent:	Ok, could you hold on please? I'll put you through to her desk.
Conference Planner:	Thank you ...
Celine:	Hello.
Conference Planner:	Is that Celine?
Celine:	Speaking.
Conference Planner:	I visited your agency last week and we talked about the tours you organize in Shanghai. You said I should get in touch with you we had made a decision.
Celine:	Oh, yes. I remember. Have you decided that you'd like to go?
Conference Planner:	Yes. I'd like to make a booking.
Celine: Fine.	I'll just get a booking form. Hold the line ... Right. Could you tell me which tour you've decided on?
Conference Planner:	The one—sorry, I haven't got the references with me—the one day one to Ningpo via the Bay Crossing Bridge.

Celine:	Ok, I'll look up the reference number later. Can you tell me what date you want to leave on?
Conference Planner:	The thirteenth of July.
Celine:	Fine. So would you mind giving me our name, please?
Conference Planner:	It's for my group of 20—Mr. White Morgan.
Celine:	Thank you, and I'll need your address.
Conference Planner:	Certainly. That's 11, High Hill, Temple Fortune, London NW116PN.
Celine:	And the telephone number?
Conference Planner:	0181 328 5252.
Celine:	Do you have a number at work?
Conference Planner:	Yes. 0171 321 5454, extension 22.
Celine:	Thanks. And are all British?
Conference Planner:	Two of us have Irish passport.
Celine:	Right. Now do you mind if I just check the details? It's Mr. White Morgan of 11, High Hill, Temple Fortune, London NW116PN. Telephone number 0181 328 5252, and at work 0171 321 5454, extension 22. departure date 13th July. Now, there's the insurance which is ...er ... is compulsory on this kind of tour. Would you like to make your own arrangements or would you rather take out the standard insurance policy?
Conference Planner:	Oh, I guess the standard one. It saves a lot of trouble.
Celine:	Yes, ok. Well the insurance premium is —wait a moment I'll look in the brochure ... um ... it's for one day, isn't it? That's ten pounds per person.
Conference Planner:	Ok.
Celine:	I'll send you a confirmation next week.
Conference Planner:	Ok.
Celine:	I'll also need your deposit which is 80 pounds per head.
Conference Planner:	Right. I'll drop by the beginning of next week and make you out a check then.
Celine:	Good. Thank you for calling. Goodbye.

Question 3: Whom does the man intend to call?

Question 4: Why does the man call the travel agency?

Question 5: How many people will be in the party?

Question 6: What is the man's telephone number at work?

Question 7: On which date will the tour start?

Question 8: What is the insurance premium?

Question 9: How much should Mr. Morgan pay as a deposit?

Question 10: When will Mr. Morgan pay the deposit?

Answers:

1. C 2. C 3. B 4. C 5. D 6. A 7. D 8. A 9. B 10. B

C. Passage Dictation

An attractive social programme is organized after the conference for participants and accompanying persons.

All tours will take place only in case of not less than 10 participants. You are welcome to book the tour until June 01, 2008 through On-line registration system.

Cancellation should be made in written form only and forwarded to the Congress Service Agency Monomax PCO by e-mail or by fax.

For cancellations received before June 15, 2008 the sum of payment will be fully refunded (minus banking costs). All refunds will be proceeded after the Conference.

There are two packages. The price per person is 16 000 RUR. This price is for persons who are planning their departure from Moscow on 15.07.2008 and Includes: excursion around Moscow, 3 breakfasts and 3 lunches, English speaking guide, all entrances according to the programme, one way ticket by comfortable train from St.Petersburg to Moscow, transfer to the Moscow airport. Price per person is 20 200 RUR. This price Includes round trip tickets by comfortable train: St. Petersburg -Moscow -St.Petersburg.

Monomax PCO provides the participants with hotel accommodation in hotel "Sputnik" in Moscow.

You can book the post - conference tour and hotel accommodation in Moscow and make the payments at your online registration page at Additional Programme Section. If you have any questions, contact us by e-mail.

Section 2 Interpretation Activities

A. Sentence Interpretation

1. First, find out the equivalents of the following words.

premiere	
in-depth consideration.	
spousal	
觀鳥散步	
恢復精神	

2. Read the following to your partner for him or her to put them down in Chinese or English.

1. Garden tours are one of the main events for the international conventions.
2. Convention Tours limited, Inc. is a premiere New York City tour operator and destination management company.
3. Tour is the one aspect of a convention that is most critical and deserves serious in-depth consideration.
4. If minimum numbers are not achieved, alternative arrangements or a complete refund of the published tour price will be made.
5. We create and manage distInctive city tours, evening entertainment programs, spousal and leisure time activities in connection with meetings and conferences held in the city.
6. 旅遊的價格不應該太高。雖然價格上會損失一點，但可以在旅遊登記報名上賺回可觀的收益。
7. 旅遊活動要在下午 4 點到 4 點半之前結束並返回賓館。這樣客人便有時間放鬆，恢復精神參加晚上的活動。
8. 與會者們忙碌地參加會議的期間，保證其家屬也能夠忙著十分重要。
9. 第二天，安排了一次清早觀鳥散步，你將有機會找出居住在弗裡塞島上的 354 種鳥類。
10. 如果您的旅遊需要與官方專案中列出的旅遊專案不同，請與會議經理們聯繫。

B. Passage Interpretation

1. First, find out the equivalents of the following words.

itinerary 營業額	

2. Read the following passages to yourself and render them into Chinese or English.

● Passage 1

For those who want to extend their stay, we suggest one of the following options that will give an impression of China today. Please indicate your preference on the Registration Form. Please note that starting and finishing times as well as a full itinerary will be confirmed once the tour is booked.

● Passage 2

會議旅遊已經成為國際旅遊業中非常重要的一部分。會議旅遊正在快速地以國際化的方式發展。僅在過去的十年時間裡就有 35000 次會議活動，營業額達到 3,5 百萬歐元。歐洲，眾所周知的世界上最大的會議中心承辦了百分之六十的全球性會議。

Reference Answers

A. Sentence Interpretation

1.

premiere	首要的
in-depth consideration.	深層次考慮
spousal	家屬
觀鳥散步	Bird Watching Walk
恢復精神	freshen up

2.
1. 參觀花園是國際會議中一個主要的活動。
2. 會議旅遊有限公司是紐約市一家首要的旅遊經營與目的地管理公司。
3. 旅遊是會議活動中的最重要的一部分，同時也是需要認真地做深層次考慮的一個方面。
4. 如果報名人數不滿，我們將做其他安排，或者按照公佈的旅遊收費全額退還。
5. 結合在本市舉辦的會議和大會，我們公司開發管理與會議相關的獨具特色的都市旅遊，晚間娛樂活動以及家屬休閒活動。

6. Tour prices should not be too high. You can lose a small amount and make up the difference at registration.
7. Try to have tours back to the hotel by 4:00 to 4:30 pm. This will allow people to relax and freshen up for any evening events.
8. While all the attendees are busy in the meetings it's important to make sure the spouses stay busy too!
9. On the second day you will enjoy a morning Bird Watching Walk to seek out some of the 354 species of birds on Fraser Island.
10. If you require touring arrangements other than those offered in the official programme, please contact the Meeting Managers.

B. Passage Interpretation

1.

itinerary 營業額	旅遊線路 turnover

2.

● Passage 1

　　我們為那些希望延長逗留時間的客人提供一下幾種會後旅遊線路，客人可以從中挑選一條自己喜歡的線路。我們設計的每條線路都能夠讓您有機會瞭解今日中國。您只需在登記表中標明自己喜歡的線路即可。請您注意您一旦您做了預定，就意味著您確認了所選擇的旅遊項目的起始時間，結束時間以及整個線路。

● Passage 2

Convention tourism has developed into an essential part of the international tourism industry. It is rapidly growing internationally with more than 35,000 convention events held in the last 10 years, with a turnover more than 3.5 billion euros. And Europe, known as the largest convention center in the world, hosts more than 60 percent of global conventions.

Section 3 Speaking Activities

A. Specialized Terms

Match the expressions on the left with the best Chinese equivalent on the right.

1. sightseeing and city tour   _____ A. 包價旅遊

2. shopping trip   _____ B. 導遊陪同旅遊

3. escorted tour   _____ C. 全天遊

4. package tour   _____ D. 配戴水肺的潛水

5. full-day excursion   _____ E. 名勝景點

6. cruise ship   _____ F. 城市觀光旅遊

7. the Bund   _____ G. 遊船

8. travel brochure   _____ H. 旅遊資訊手冊

9. places of historic interests   _____ I. 外灘

10. scuba-diving   _____ J. 購物旅遊

B. Sample Conversation

Listen and read aloud.

Situation: Mr. Lee comes to Spring Travel Service to have a detailed talk about the post-conference tour of Shanghai with Mr. Liu, clerk of the Spring Travel Service.

Mr. Liu: Is there anything I can do for you?

Mr. Lee: Yes. My friends told me Beijing is so wonderful a city. I want to see it with my own eyes. Can you suggest something?

Mr. Liu: Many places in Beijing are worth seeing. Why not start with Tiananmen Square?

Mr. Lee: Then what?

Mr. Liu: You may go to Beihai(North Sea) Park.

Mr. Lee: I'm an architect. Are there any emperor tombs I can see around?

Mr. Liu: Certainly. I suggest you going Ming Tombs.

Mr. Lee: How can I get there?

Mr. Liu: To save time, you can take a taxi.

Mr. Lee: But I want a tour guide to escort me.

Mr. Liu: In that case, a package tour will be fine with you.

Mr. Lee: You're so thoughtful. Could you arrange this tour for me?

Mr. Liu: Yes, just a moment.

C. Functional Expressions

Read aloud and practice with your partner.

Could you tell me some places of historical interest in Shanghai?

They are within easy access. The City Sightseeing Bus No. 7 will take you there in succession. You may go out of the hotel, turn right, and you'll find the bus stop at the corner of the street.

Lunch will at 12 o'clock at the Spring Restaurant near the Lake.

Our guides are capable of both English and French, but bilingual service costs more.

We charge RMB 300 yuan per person per day, excluding the meals.

D. Speaking Up

Translate the following sentences into English by using as many language skills learnt as possible.

1. ——_____?

——I'm very pleased to suggest that you go to the Yu Yuan Garden and the Shanghai Old Street.

（用意：詢問旅遊景點）

2. ——Could you tell me how to go to these places?

—— _____.

（用意：介紹路線）

3. ——What about the meals?

—— _____.

（用意：介紹用餐安排）

4. ——I want a tour guide to escort our group.

—— _____.

（用意：介紹導遊服務）

5. ——How much does the tour cost?

_____ _____.

（用意：報價）

1. Could you tell me some places of historical interest in Shanghai?
2. They are within easy access. The City Sightseeing Bus No. 7 will take you there in succession. You may go out of the hotel, turn right, and you'll find the bus stop at the corner of the street.
3. Lunch will at 12 o'clock at the Spring Restaurant near the Lake.
4. Our guides are capable of both English and French, but bilingual service costs more.
5. We charge 300 yuan RMB person per day, excluding the meals.

E. Role-play

Practice the following in English according to the situations.

• Situation 1

At the travel desk, a travel Reservationist reserves a one-day post-conference city tour of Shanghai for Mr. Hilton, a meeting planner of a group of 28 members. The planner asks questions to find out necessary information. The clerk makes responses if necessary. You play the role of Mr. Hilton.

Your questions:

Which three places does a one day city tour Include?
What can we expect to see in each of these places?
How long wills the tour last?
How much does the tour cost per person?
Can we hire a tour guide capable of speaking both English and French?
How much do you charge for the tour guide?

• Situation 2

A: You are a clerk of Convention Tours Limited Inc Shanghai. Your company is in charge of creating and managing the tour of the annual meeting of America Bankers Association. A potential guest calls for information about post convention tour registration. Please use the case given to answer the call.

B:　You are an attendee of the annual meeting of America Bankers Association. You are calling to enquire about tour alternatives, price, and other details about the post convention tour.

Reference Answer

A. Specialized Terms

1. F 2. J 3. B 4. A 5. C 6. G 7. I 8. H 9. E 10. D

D. Speaking Up

1. Could you tell me some places of historical interest in Shanghai?

2. They are within easy access. The City Sightseeing Bus No. 7 will take you there in succession. You may go out of the hotel, turn right, and you'll find the bus stop at the corner of the street.

3. Lunch will at 12 o'clock at the Spring Restaurant near the Lake.

4. Our guides are capable of both English and French, but bilingual service costs more.

5. We charge 300 yuan RMB person per day, excluding the meals.

Chapter 15
Event Review Meetings 會後總結

▍Section 1 Listening Activities

Learn these words and expressions before starting to listen to the tape.

panel		n.	小組
barcode		n.	條碼
tentative		a.	嘗試的
outlet		n.	出口
protruding		a.	向外突出的
bump		v.	碰撞
simultaneous interpretation		n.	同聲傳譯
acoustics		n.	聲學效果
make or break			顯著成功或徹底失敗
feedback			回饋
promotional campaign			促銷運動

A. Spot Dictation

Tonight I participated in a (1) _____ about what's coming in 2008. It was hosted by Ember Media and overall I'd say it was one of the most enjoyable evenings I've had in a while. The (2) _____ before, during and after the panel was great. It's always great to meet people in person who read CN.

The Ember Media team did an excellent job (3) _____ as everything went off without a hitch. Clayton Banks, Ember Media CEO led off with a presentation about his picks for 2008. The truth is that 2008 might be the most exciting year on the Web yet. We may (4) _____ ___ than we have in the last 3-4 years combined.

The panel discussion (5) _____: Jonah Bossewitch, Kay Madati and myself. Jonah works at Columbia University and Kay runs marketing for Community Connect (6) _____ which did half a billion pageviews in December 2007.

Some of the topics (7) _____

_____, data portability, mobile, (8) _____

_____.

Thanks to Clayton for Including me and thanks to everyone for coming out.

B. Multiple Choices

Directions: *In this section you will hear several Dialogue. After each Dialogue, there are some questions. Listen to the Dialogue carefully and choose the most appropriate answer to each question from the four choices marked A, B, C and D.*

• Dialogue 1

1. What time of the day does the Mr. Johnson come to the venuc?

   A. On the morning.

   B. On the afternoon.

   C. In the evening.

   D. At noon.

2. On which day does Mr. Johnson come to the venue?

   A. On the event day.

   B. On the day after the event.

   C. On the day before the event.

   D. Two days before the event.

3. What is the most probable relationship between Mr. Johnson and Mr. Brown?

   A. Meeting planner and exhibitor

   B. Meeting planner and meeting manager

   C. Meeting manager and exhibitor

   D. Meeting manager and sponsor

4. Who will accompany Mr. Johnson?

   A. Mr. Brown and his staff

   B. Mr. Brown and all area managers

   C. Mr. Brown's staff and all area managers

   D. All area managers

● **Dialogue 2**

5. What is the most probable relationship between the two speakers?

   A. General manager and staff.

   B. Event planner and manager.

   C. Event planner and secretary.

   D. General manager and secretary.

6. What kind of event will Peter's organization hold at the venue?

   A. Exhibition.

   B. Exhibition and meeting.

   C. Meeting.

   D. Trade show.

7. How many outlets did Peter check in person?

   A. All.

   B. About 5%.

   C. About 15%.

   D. About 50%.

8. When was this meeting held?

   A. Long before the event.

   B. After the event.

   C. On the day before the event.

   D. In the process of the event.

● **Dialogue 3**

9. What are Dr. Pan and his students talking about?

   A. They are talking about microphones.

   B. They are talking about loudspeakers.

   C. They are talking about the sound system.

   D. They are talking about brand-named equipment.

10. We can learn from the Dialogue that poor sound can _____.

   A. damage people's ears

   B. cause stress

   C. cause fatigue

D. cause both stress and fatigue

11. The factors that influence sound quality Include   .

   A. room acoustics, loudspeakers and earphones

   B. room acoustics, earphones, and sound equipment

   C. loudspeakers, earphones and sound equipment

   D. room acoustics, loudspeakers, earphones and sound equipment

12. According to Dr. Pan, what is the crucial factor of a event?

   A. Details.

   B. Sound system.

   C. Sound equipment.

   D. Details and equipment.

C. Passage Dictation

Directions: *In this section, you will hear a passage. Listen carefully and write down what you hear on the tape.*

Tape script:

_____

_____

_____

_____

_____

_____

_____

_____

_____

_____

Tape script & Answers

A. Spot Dictation

Tape script:

Tonight I participated in a (1) <u>panel discussion</u> about what's coming in 2008. It was hosted by Ember Media and overall I'd say it was one of the most enjoyable evenings I've had in a while. The (2) <u>conversation</u> before, during and after the panel was great. It's always great to meet people in person who read CN.

The Ember Media team did an excellent job (3) <u>in coordination and organization</u> as everything went off without a hitch. Clayton Banks, Ember Media CEO led off with a presentation about his picks for 2008. The truth is that 2008 might be the most exciting year on the Web yet. We may (4) <u>move further along overall this year</u> than we have in the last 3-4 years combined.

The panel discussion (5) <u>followed with panelists</u>: Jonah Bossewitch, Kay Madati and myself. Jonah works at Columbia University and Kay runs marketing for <u>Community Connect</u> (6) <u>which Includes sites such as Black Planet</u> which did half a billion page views in December 2007.

Some of the topics (7) <u>we discussed Include: online advertising, supply/demand with regards to content, privacy</u>, data portability, mobile, (8) <u>barcode technology with regards to advertising and the semantic Web</u>.

Thanks to Clayton for Including me and thanks to everyone for coming out.

B. Multiple Choices

Tape script:

• **Dialogue 1**

Man: 1:　Good morning, Mr. Johnson. Welcome to our venue.

Man: 2:　Thank you, Mr. Brown. I'd like to walk through the venue to be sure everything is made ready for tomorrow's event.

Man: 1:　I will go with you in person, together with the heads of all work areas.

Man: 2:　It is very considerate of you. Their presence will save me a lot of time if any problem will be found.

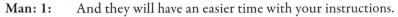

Man: 1: And they will have an easier time with your instructions.

Man: 2: Let's get going.

● Dialogue 2

Man: 1: Good afternoon, everyone. Let's start the meeting now. First, I'd like to express my sIncere thanks to your careful and tentative arrangement for our event. All of you here have worked three days unstopped setting up and installing all necessary equipment. In order to guarantee the event a success, however, I have to say that we still need to do a little more. I did a walkthrough this morning and found that some equipment is still not installed, and some, although installed, are not proper.

Woman: Oh? Peter, please just be frank.

Man: 1: I am, Tony. I checked 15% of the outlets and I found, unfortunately, some just do not work.

Woman: Ben, you are in charge of this area. Can you explain?

Man: 2: Yes, Miss. I will look into it after the meeting.

Man: 1: And the headphone plug. It is not secure, actually a little protruding. You know, if so, it will get bumped or caught in clothing, maybe.

Woman: Mark, make sure that your men will get these things right as soon as possible.

Man: 2: Yes, sir. We will get them right and make them work properly through out the convention.

● Dialogue 3

Woman 1: Dr. Pan, can you tell us something about sound systems at a booth, or in a meeting hall?

Man: That's a Good question. Well, actually, sound is fairly important. It is directly related to the success of a event.

Woman 1: Yes, I heard that Good sound quality in the booth and at a conference is an essential factor. It is especially important for simultaneous interpretation.

Woman 2: I can't agree more. Poor sound causes unnecessary stress and fatigue. But how can we ensure Good sound quality?

Man: Good sound depends on Many factors, Including proper sound equipment that supplies a full range of sound.

Woman 1: Also room acoustics.

Woman 2: And loudspeakers distributed around the room. But the volume must be kept low enough

Man: Yes, and lightweight earphones can't be skipped. You see?

Woman 1&2: Yes, sir.

Man: The main point is that you should forever remember that it is details that make or break an event.

Woman 1: So, why?

Man: Let's take microphones as an example. If the microphone is fixed to the control panel, it should have a long enough flexible stem so the interpreter is not forced to adopt a rigid or awkward position.

Woman 2: And I think it is important to apply brand-name equipment.

Man: You said it. Actually, the best advice in a constantly changing situation is to consult the THC on what is currently the best available equipment.

Answers:

A 2. C 3. B 4. B 5. B 6. C 7. C 8. C 9. C 10. D 11. D 12. A

C. Passage Dictation

Tape script:

Event evaluation is necessary to make you and your team more efficient and effective, the next time you organize an event. It is all about finding your mistakes and learning from them. Event evaluation should be done immediately after the event is over or the next day. Conduct a meeting with your team members to evaluate your event.

Determine the extent to which event and advertising objectives have been achieved. If you are not able to achieve your event and advertising objectives through your event, then no matter how much people enjoyed the event or how much popularity your event got, it is a complete failure on a commercial level.

Create an event evaluation report. The event evaluation report is the documentation of the activities carried out during the event evaluation. Whatever you did during the event evaluation will be a part of this report. It means this report will Include the actual filled feedback forms from the clients and the target audience; problems identified and discussed during meeting; solutions to various identified problems; performance evaluation report of the team members and the service providers; promotional campaign analysis report etc.

Section 2 Interpretation Activities

A. Sentence Interpretation

1. First, find out the equivalents of the following words.

session address 會務費	

2. Read the following to your partner for him or her to put them down in Chinese or English.

1. When a convention program draws to a close, you will have the opportunity to review and assess the experience and satisfaction level of the convention event.

2. Sister Cities International and the Conference Planning Committee will consider your comments carefully when planning future events.

3. Please take a few moments to answer the following questions so we may improve upon future programs.

4. I also think a 3-day session would provide more time for the type of one on one interaction, as well as further small group discussions.

5. Although I agree with many of the positive overall comments about the Conference, I also believe there were some shortcomings that I would like to address.

6. 我認為會務費價格太高。

7. 有關此次會議的一些優缺點下面會詳細列出。希望這些在以後的行業會議中會有所改變。

8. 學習 2005 是一次非常成功的會議，但是由於行業的特點，仍然缺少了一些基本要素。

9. 請您用一點時間就此次分會提出任何其他的意見並對未來會議提出您的建議。

10. 當聽到每一位發言人的發言簡介幾乎雷同時，我真的感覺非常鬱悶。

B. Passage Interpretation

1. First, find out the equivalents of the following words.

回訪溝通函	

2. Read the following passages to yourself and render them into Chinese or English.

● Passage 1

    Thank you for completing the conference evaluations. We appreciate that you have taken the time to help the Global Health Council improve their Annual Conference. Your opinions, comments and suggestions are important to us. There are two different types of evaluations that can be completed. Option 1 is General Conference Evaluations and Option 2 is Specific Session Evaluation. You can do both of them or choose one. Thank you!

● Passage 2

    銷售發生在展覽結束後，所以你應該準備好一套回訪策略。寄發回訪溝通函，撥打回訪電話和銷售電話。展覽結束後還要實施銷售，三個月後要總結銷售成果。你將會吃驚地發現參加一次工業展示會受益良多。

Reference Answers

A. Sentence Interpretation

1.

session	會期
address	強調，指出
會務費	conference admission fee

2.

1. 會議接近尾聲時，你就有機會回顧與評估會議活動的經驗和滿意度。
2. 國際姐妹城市與會議策劃委員會策劃未來活動時會認真考慮您的意見。
3. 請您用幾分鐘時間回答下面幾個問題以便我們在未來活動中有所改進。
4. 我認為安排為期 3 天的分會可以提供更多一對一互動的時間，也可有更多時間開展小組討論。

5. 雖然我很同意許多就這次會議所做出的肯定評價，但我認為仍然存在一些缺點需要指出。

6. I think the price was rather high for the conference admission.

7. Some of the Good and bad points of the conference are detailed below. They are provided to encourage changes in all future industry conferences.

8. Learning 2005 was a very successful conference, but as is typical in our industry this conference still lacked some fundamental elements.

   a) Please take a moment to provide any additional comments about the session and suggestions for future meetings.

   b) I was really getting frustrated when I heard that almost every speaker prefaces his presentation with essentially the same comments.

B. Passage Interpretation

1.

回訪溝通函	follow-up communications

2.

● Passage 1

謝謝您填寫會議評價表。我們感謝您抽出時間幫助世界健康委員會改進其年度會議。您的觀點，意見以及建議對我們十分重要。有兩種評估辦法可供您選擇。一種是會議總體評價，另一種是具體分會評價。您可選擇一種填寫，或者也可兩者均做。謝謝！

● Passage 2

Sales are made after the show, so you should have a follow-up strategy in place! Send out follow-up communications, make follow-up phone and sales calls. Qualify sales post event and review the results in three months time - you'll be surprised how many will be attributed to your presence at a trade show.

Section 3 Speaking Activities

A. Specialized Terms

Match the expressions on the left with the best Chinese equivalent on the right.

● **Part 1**

1. project manager	_____A. 籌備期
2. Expo-format	_____B. 框架展台
3. capacity	_____C. 參展商
4. attendance	_____D. 專用洽談區
5. exhibitor	_____E. 反採購
6. professional visitor	_____F. 接待能力
7. lead time	_____G. 海外參展商
8. shell scheme	_____H. 專案經理
9. first-tier supplier	_____I. 參展人數
10. reversed on-site purchasing	_____J. 專業觀眾
11. one-on-one meeting room	_____K. 一級供應商
12. overseas exhibitor	_____L. 展會形式

● **Part 2**

1. dimmer	A. 講壇，講台
2. carousel projector	B. 接線板
3. spotlight	C. 遠端電信會議
4. roaming microphone	D. 寫字紙
5. teleprompter	E. 幻燈機
6. flip chart	F. 漫遊式麥克風
7. LCD panel	G. 聚光燈
8. easel	H. 夜晶顯示幕
9. podium	I. 三腳架
10. head receiver	J. 電視提詞器
11. house board	K. 頭戴式耳機
12. teleconference	L. 燈光調節器

B. Sample Conversation

Listen and read aloud.

Situation: Mr. Shelton, the convention service manager of Grand Hotel is hosting the evaluation meeting of the annual meeting of American Association of real estate. Mr. Smith, the meeting planner of the Association is presenting the meeting on behalf on the association.

CSM: Shall we start the evaluation meeting now, Mr. Smith?

MP: Is everyone who attended the pre-convention meeting here, Mr. Shelton?

CSM: Yes, Mr. Smith. All the directors are here. Catering director, F&B director, and the director of Security, Front Office Manager, Reservation Manager and our sales executive. They are all present.

MP: Well, let's start. First please allow me to give you all my heartfelt thanks. Your hard work and attentive service made our convention a great success. Our thanks especially go to the catering staff who provided our attendees with nice food of both western and Chinese styles.

CD: Thank you Mr. Smith. I'm very glad to hear that. It's our honor to serve you and our staff is looking forward to serving you again soon.

MP: I hope so. But I have to point out that two of our attendees complained the slow procedure of luggage delivery.

FOM: I'm sorry for it. But, Mr. Smith, you know yours is a big group. So it kept our bellman fairly busy to try to send the luggage to guests' room quickly enough. Unfortunately, we failed to notice that the two guests were rather tired. But we did try to make it up by offering them some refreshments on house.

MP: Thanks to your thoughtfulness and the two guests actually were deeply impressed by your attentive and friendly service later.

SE: We are so happy to know that all your attendees enjoyed their stay at our hotel. And we hope that we can have your next convention.

MP: It was just what I was thinking about, given your satisfactory security and reservation services. But I was wondering if you could low down the bill little. Our sponsor thinks that cost on equipment is still too high.

SE: But the equipment we provided with your convention is all brand-new most updated.

MP: I have to say that I can't agree more on this aspect. Your sound system did contribute a lot to the success of our convention. Beside this, I still think there is some room for lowing the bill down.

CSM: Then we can give you 30% discount if you let us do all your annual meetings.

MP: What about 50% if we give you all our annual meetings and seasonal meetings?

CSM: Thank you, Mr. Smith. We will try our best to make each of your meetings a great success.

C. Functional Expressions

Talking about similarities and differences

They had more exhibitors than those to be expected of ours.

Comparing all the previous Auto Expos, the biggest difference is size.

The Supertechnology Show is more expensive than Power Coating Europe.

There are four times as many exhibitors at CES as at Coating Europe.

Another difference is that these shows represent two separate markets for us.

The main similarity is that many of the big name companies will be exhibiting at both Expos.

What the buyer will achieve will equal to that at 30 traditional exhibitions.

Talking about advantages and disadvantages

Would it be more appropriate to ...

The only drawback is ...

How is ...going for you?

Comparing the two shows, ...

You're absolutely right, but the problem is ...

The main advantage of ... is ...

D. Speaking Up

1. 參加本屆展會的參展商人數是去年的四倍。
2. 本應該為採購參展商事先安排與供應商一對一的洽談。
3. 參加本次展覽的一大好處是我們見到了來自世界各地的零售商。
4. 但是，另一方面，我們本該多提供一些場地。

5. 展會唯一的不足是成本太高了。

E. Role-play

Practice the conversation in English according to the situation.

● **Situation**

You are Mr. William Thompson, the meeting planner of the Global Education council. You are presenting the post convention meeting summarizing the Good and bad points of the 45th annual conference of the council that was headquartered at Holiday Inn Tibet.

Reference Answer

A. Specialized Terms

● **Part 1**

1. H 2. L 3. F 4. I 5. C 6. J 7. A 8. B 9. K 10. E 11. D 12. G

● **Part 2**

1. L 2. E 3. G 4. F 5. J 6. D 7. H 8. I 9. A 10. K 11. B 12. C

D. Speaking Up

1. There are four times as many exhibitors at the expo as last time.
2. Sourcing exhibitors should have been prearranged for one-on-one meetings with suppliers.
3. One big advantage of attending this exhibiting is that we have met retailers from all over the country.
4. But on the other hand, we could have offered larger exhibition area.
5. The only drawback of this expo is the cost.

國家圖書館出版品預行編目（CIP）資料

會展實用英語（聽說口譯篇）/ 吳雲主編 . -- 第一版 . -- 臺
北市：崧博出版：崧燁文化發行 , 2019.05
　　面；　公分
POD 版

ISBN 978-957-735-719-9（平裝）

1. 商業英文 2. 讀本

805.18　　　　　　　　　　　　　　　　　108002904

書　　名：會展實用英語（聽說口譯篇）

作　　者：吳雲 主編

發 行 人：黃振庭

出 版 者：崧博出版事業有限公司

發 行 者：崧燁文化事業有限公司

E - m a i l：sonbookservice@gmail.com

粉絲頁：　　　　　　　網址：

地　　址：台北市中正區重慶南路一段六十一號八樓 815 室

8F.-815, No.61, Sec. 1, Chongqing S. Rd., Zhongzheng

Dist., Taipei City 100, Taiwan (R.O.C.)

電　　話：(0(2)2370-3310 傳　真：(0(2) 2370-3210

總 經 銷：紅螞蟻圖書有限公司

地　　址：台北市內湖區舊宗路二段 121 巷 19 號

電　　話:02-2795-3656 傳真 :02-2795-4100　　網址：

印　　刷：京峯彩色印刷有限公司（京峰數位）

定　　價：400 元

發行日期：2019 年 05 月第一版

◎ 本書以 POD 印製發行